One shot to
prove my skills in bed

With the one woman
who can't stand me

What can possibly
go wrong?

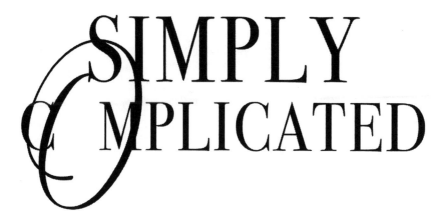

SIMPLY COMPLICATED

S. NELSON

To those who finally got their happily ever after

OLIVIA

"I can't tell if you're serious or not." Brooke, my best friend, narrowed her eyes at me before pursing her lips in that cute yet marginally annoying way of hers. "Sounds more like something I would do. Not you. Besides, you've never had one."

"I know, that's the point." I tapped the side of my glass with the tip of my fingernail, gearing up for the upcoming conversation. Some might refer to what I wanted to do as careless. Others might view it as bold. But I preferred liberating.

"I meant you've never had a one-night stand. You're a serial monogamist." Her smile amused and irritated me simultaneously.

"Am not." A quick flick of her brow caused me to stammer over my next words. "Okay... maybe... hell, you're right. To be fair, though, things just happened to work out that way."

"Because you choose relationships over letting go and having fun."

She signaled to the bartender for a refill as she drained the remainder of her wine. He practically tripped over himself to get to her, ignoring the two guys who'd been waiting patiently to be served. Little did he know she was only interested in women. Sometimes that tidbit of information caused some guys to pursue her even more, which I thought was odd since they didn't stand a chance.

Brooke never made a big announcement she was a lesbian. Anyone who knew her was aware. She didn't hide it, not from her parents, her friends, or her classmates when we were in school. Her sexual identity was part of her, as it was for the rest of us. When I stumbled across her kissing Jenny Madsen behind the gymnasium in seventh grade, she winked at me. Jenny, on the other hand, made us both promise we wouldn't say anything to anyone, telling us her parents would be so mad if they found out. Brooke, being the self-assured person she was, even at twelve years old, rolled her eyes at the poor girl and told her she was missing out.

I'd been jealous of her confidence. Still was to this day. She didn't care what anyone thought about her, living her best life every single day. Brooke wasn't perfect, and she had problems like the rest of us, but her attitude toward life, and believing everything would work out, was something to be admired.

"I want to be more like you," I joked, the underlying seriousness of my jest peeking through.

"Who doesn't?" Her shoulders bounced in a lazy shrug. "Seriously, though, I'm all for you trying this out, but promise me you'll be safe. There are a lot of creeps looking to take advantage of someone as innocent as yourself."

"You make it sound like I have no idea what I'm doing." I couldn't decide if I was offended or not. "I'm not inexperienced."

A small commotion erupted across the bar, and when I turned to see what happened, there was a small crowd gathered near the door. The group of patrons seemed excited, but I couldn't determine why.

"Having three long-term boyfriends doesn't exactly qualify you as experienced," Brooke said, poking my shoulder to get my attention. "You met all of them through friends or in school. You don't know what it's like to pick up men."

"Neither do you."

"True, but I've had plenty of them hit on me, and I'm much better at detecting bullshit than you are." She playfully nudged my arm. "You're too trusting."

My lips parted in preparation to disagree, but as the words filtered through my brain, I was aware whatever I spewed back at her would be a lie.

She was right.

I believed everyone to have the best intentions because that was how I was. It was only over the past year that my blinders had started to fade away. I supposed I could thank Cody, my recent ex, for exposing me to some of the harsh realities of life. Correction, to the harsh realities of loving someone who was selfish and ended up being an overall prick.

The trust in our relationship dwindled when I caught him texting some girl six months ago, someone he vehemently denied cheating with. I didn't wholeheartedly believe him, but I didn't *not* believe him either, if that made any sense. After the incident, he became unusually possessive and controlling toward me, which was a sure sign he was, in fact, doing something he wasn't supposed to be. And even though I couldn't link the connection at the time, I knew in my gut something was off.

I wasted a year and a half on that relationship, and most days the thought of him angered me. But there were times when his image would infiltrate, and sadness would creep over me. And it was during those instances when I stalked his social media. Nine times out of ten I'd remind myself he wasn't worth it, and my inner chastisement would work. But for the one time it didn't, I was left feeling a certain way. Not depressed, because I didn't want to be with him, but possibly insulted I was replaced so quickly. I ended things with him four months ago, and he was already in a three-month-long relationship.

Wanting to skip over whatever else Brooke had in store in ways of warning me away from what I wanted to do, I brought the conversation back around.

"Back to my point, please," I said, elongating the last word for emphasis. A subtle nod from my bestie was all I needed to continue. I leaned in closer to make sure whatever I divulged was kept as private as could be, considering we were in a crowded bar, the blended voices of the customers providing a shield to our conversation. Or at least, I hoped that was the case. "I'm curious if it'll happen with a stranger, someone I have no feelings for whatsoever. Someone I'll only be with one time, you know, to take the pressure off, which is what I believe might be the issue. Not that I've thought about it too much." *It's all I've been thinking about recently.*

After a long exhale I continued my rant, crouching so close to Brooke she had to inch back a little. "You gush over your sexcapades, bragging about how many times it happens for you. I'm jealous."

"Sexcapades?" She tapped her finger against her bottom lip. "I like it. I'm gonna steal that one."

"Be my guest." Tipping my glass to take a drink, I almost missed my mouth completely when whoever took the seat next to me jostled my arm. A "sorry" drifted through the air next to me, but I never turned to see who the apology came from, too engrossed in my interaction with my friend. "I want to at least give it a try."

"What are you going to do? Pick up some random guy and ask if he'll help you out?"

"No, not exactly. I'd rather he be a friend of a friend. I need to know he's not a psycho."

"Yeah, you don't want that."

"Exactly." A small sip of wine passed my lips, sliding down my throat and adding to the feel-good vibe I had going on. "My only other requirements are that he's attractive and knows how to use what he's got." I moved to stretch my back. "Oh, and I want someone who's a good kisser." I wasn't sure if it was how I said it or my expression, but Brooke laughed.

"Kiss you where?"

"Very funny. You know what I mean." Unloading all of this on her was liberating, like a secret I'd been holding on to was finally set free. "I'd even be willing to pay him for his time and effort."

"Pay him?" she asked, her voice raising a notch.

"Shh." I smacked her arm, too embarrassed at the thought someone heard to look anywhere but directly at her. I lowered my voice when I spoke again just in case someone *was* eaves-dropping. "Yes. I'd be willing to compensate him because he'd be doing me a favor."

"Honey, you'd be doing any guy a favor if you simply looked at him, let alone propositioned him. Sex with a hot chick with no commitments? What guy would turn that down?"

"But I don't want a quickie, where he's the only one to get off. I want to have an orgasm too. That's the whole point of this, for him to work at it, to work with me to make sure I have one. And since I've failed every other time I've tried to during sex, it might take a while, if it'll happen at all."

"Regardless of how much work it might take, any guy would jump at the chance. You know they love a challenge. Trust me. There won't be a need to pay anyone."

My shoulders came up to my ears before dropping. "Well, I'd be willing to if need be."

Brooke tucked an errant strand of her chocolate-colored hair behind her ear, her eyes skating over my face several times. "You're dead serious, aren't you?"

"Yup. I want in."

"In?"

"To the club."

"What club?"

I made it a point to keep my voice low. It was embarrassing enough I couldn't come during sex, the last thing I needed was for some stranger to be privy to the information.

"The orgasm club."

My friend repeated what I'd said, louder than I appreciated.

"You're too much, Liv."

"Says the woman who comes every time."

"What's the point otherwise?"

"Exactly." I took another sip of my drink before placing the wineglass back on top of the bar. For as much as I loved to talk a good game, I had little faith in myself of actually going through with propositioning a stranger. And if that were the case, I'd have to resign myself to the fate of never having an orgasm during sex for the rest of my life. Hell, I could barely get myself off most times.

It wasn't that I couldn't feel pleasure, because I could, but I couldn't push past a certain point. Then I'd get frustrated and just give up.

"I need to pee. Are you going to be all right by yourself for a few minutes? Don't interview anyone without me," she teased before I could answer her question, adjusting the bottom of her denim skirt before walking toward the back of the bar.

While I waited for Brooke to return, I thought about what I'd said. I was completely serious when I divulged my plan, but talking about it and doing something about it were two different things. Being adventurous was something I aspired to. But was that really me? I wanted to answer yes, but I was still figuring myself out. And there was nothing like a cheating ex to put a damper on someone's self-esteem.

My phone alerted me to an incoming message from my mother. I wasn't in the right frame of mind to read it, though. She was no doubt texting to ask if I was coming to dinner tomorrow night. She'd told me the other day she had a surprise for me, and I knew exactly what that meant. After my breakup, she'd managed to set me up on two blind dates, both of whom were sons of her nursing friends she worked with at the hospital.

She'd remind me I wasn't getting any younger, as if twenty-six was old, and that I needed to meet someone and settle down, so I'd have enough time to have kids. I argued I'd meet someone when I was ready, but it was as if whatever I said went in one ear and out the other, her mom brain refusing to accept maybe it wasn't in the cards for her youngest child to give her grandkids.

Her reasoning for not hounding my brother, Mark, like she did me was that it was different for men. He had more time than I did. Some bullshit about biological clocks.

It was during those times I'd look to my dad for help, but he was no better. He didn't trick me into dates I didn't want, but he'd say something like "humor your mother" or "she might be on to something."

With my body angled toward the hallway where Brooke disappeared, and my attention on a second text alert chime, I was startled when someone brushed up behind me, warm breath cascading over the shell of my ear.

"I'd be happy to help you out with your dilemma."

The hairs on the back of my neck bristled, and it had nothing to do with my embarrassment at having someone confirm they'd indeed heard what I'd told Brooke. But instead had everything to do with who the voice belonged to.

Someone I hadn't laid eyes on in ten years.

Someone who had broken my heart once upon a time.

Someone I despised.

2

OLIVIA

My first inclination was to ignore him, hoping he'd go away. But if I remembered anything about the guy behind me, it was that he loved to get under my skin, and not always in a good way. If he was still the same stubborn, arrogant, and infuriating person I knew a decade ago, there was no way he was going to let me off the hook. He'd view me as too much of a challenge now to walk away on his own.

"Don't ignore me, Ollie. I know you heard what I said."

Instead of focusing on the rasp of his voice, which was slightly deeper than the last time I heard it, I homed in on the nickname he gave me all those years ago, one I didn't care for. I whipped around in my seat to face him, prepared to tell him off, but the second I laid eyes on him, all my bravado flitted away. For the briefest of moments, I was catapulted back to that sixteen-year-old girl who'd been infatuated with her neighbor, her brother's best friend. A guy she thought she loved, until he broke her heart.

Silently screaming at myself to get it together, I steeled my posture and raised my head high. There was no way I was going to allow him to see me sweat.

"You know I hate that nickname."

"I know."

One minute I wanted to wipe the smirk off his face, and the next I wanted him to say something else that would make his mouth curve into that sexy grin again.

Various thoughts battled for me to give them life, but they were so random I barely had time to digest them before they were gone, only to be replaced with another odd one. When I finally settled on something appropriate to say, I parted my lips, but then snapped them shut. The slight rise of his brow showcased his amusement, and it was in that moment I realized no matter what I said, good or bad, he was only going to banter with me. Which meant, he'd only serve to rile me further.

So I stayed quiet. But there was nothing that said I couldn't return his stare. As his eyes traveled over me, mine did the same to him. The last time I saw him in person, he was only eighteen. His dark hair had been cropped close to his head and he was clean shaven. He'd been gorgeous, but no comparison to the man he'd become.

His hair was longer now, a mass of unruly waves on top that worked perfectly on him. His jaw was covered with a trimmed beard, highlighting his full lips. He looked more rugged, all while still maintaining an ounce of the boy he used to be. One thing was still the same, minus the fine lines around the edges. His eyes were as piercing as they'd ever been, the shade switching from light blue to hazel to even gray, depending on the lighting. It was those eyes that had once promised me everything I didn't even know I wanted. Eyes I couldn't trust now for fear all the hurt and humiliation I'd felt back then would bubble back to the surface.

Seeing him after all this time was surreal. Sure, I'd seen plenty of images of him. There was no escaping one of the million pictures plastered online. The man offering to "help me out" was none other than the famous American Soccer League player, Luke Sorenson. He'd been to the Olympics several times during his career, winning gold and silver medals with his team. Except for myself, women loved him, and men wanted to be him.

But I knew him when he was nothing more than a guy obsessed with the sport, playing for his high school team before being given a scholarship to UCLA.

Now he was rich and famous. Was there any higher goal to accomplish? *How about not being an insensitive asshole?*

I digressed. I'd relive the pain he'd caused me, and our little run-in wouldn't turn out in anyone's favor if I didn't stop. Of that, I was sure.

After what felt like an hour of us studying the other, I moved to turn back around, deciding it was best if I didn't engage any further. But I barely swung my seat an inch before his hand was on my knee.

"What do you think you're doing? Take your hand off me."

"Are you sure?"

"Absolutely." My tone was riddled with irritation. "And just so there's no misunderstanding. I don't need your help with anything." He was too slow in removing his hand, so I swatted it away, refusing to admit his touch did strange things to me.

"That's not true. If what you told Brooke wasn't a lie, you most definitely need my help." He licked his lips and leaned in close. "And I'd do it from the goodness of my heart. You wouldn't even have to pay me."

A rush of heat swirled through me, and I had no doubt my cheeks were now flushed. But what I couldn't figure out was if the warmth was from anger or frustration or embarrassment. Perhaps it was a mixture of all three.

"Thanks, but no thanks. Besides, I wouldn't want to be a notch on *that* belt. By now, it's probably worn out, ready to fall off." I mentally high-fived myself for my quick wit.

SIMPLY COMPLICATED | 11

"If that's your way of asking me if I have a disease, I can assure you I don't. But if that was your way of muddling through a weird colloquialism... umm... I have no words." His tone was a mix of condescension, amusement, and a bit of offensiveness blended in for good measure.

"Let's pretend we never saw each other. You go back to doing whatever it is you're doing, and I'll enjoy the rest of my night."

As if the universe knew I needed help, three women approached and sidled up to him, asking if he would take selfies with them. He obliged, looking first to me. A quick roll of my eyes made him smile for some reason, but I wasn't about to ask why because that would mean more interaction with him.

I wanted to ignore the spectacle, but all I could do was stare at the way he grinned at each one of them, a rush of heat blooming in my belly when the short blonde woman pressed her lips to his cheek. Refusing to acknowledge I was jealous, because the notion was simply ridiculous, I chalked up whatever feeling held me captive as the result of the wine I'd been consuming.

Once the women left, Luke scooted his barstool closer, spreading his legs wide as he faced me. I didn't want to, but I looked at his crotch, and I hadn't torn my gaze away fast enough because he caught me red-handed. Surprisingly, he didn't call me out on my brazenness, though.

"I don't want to pretend I didn't see you," he continued, like our conversation hadn't just been interrupted. A sentiment I couldn't readily identify whirled through his voice, one which had me rooted in place, questioning whether he was messing with me or being sincere.

"Well... I... um...." My words trailed off as I shrugged, not knowing what else to say. I'd only been near him a short while, and already he had me all flustered.

"Can I make my argument on why you should let me help you out? If you don't like it, I'll leave you alone."

His teeth toyed with his bottom lip while he waited for me to answer. The problem was, I didn't want to rush to say no this time, even though that was probably going to be my answer in the end. I thought about his question for a full fifteen seconds before responding, and as I suspected, a two-letter word forced its way up my throat.

"No."

"No, what?" Brooke asked, shoving me toward Luke so she could hop back onto her seat.

I didn't need to answer because he did it for me, leaning forward to catch her eye.

"Hi, Brooke. How are you?"

Her mouth dropped open right before she shoved against me once more, hopping off her seat to give him a hug.

"Oh my God! Luke! What are you doing here?"

I never told her he was moving back here from Miami to play for the Vegas United FC, information I'd unwillingly received from my dad.

Her excitement at seeing him irked me, but it shouldn't have because she had no idea what happened between us when we were younger. She was aware I used to have a crush on him, but that was all she knew. I told my best friend everything, except what happened that night. I was too humiliated to speak a word of it, pushing the memory into the recesses of my mind. Now and again, the recollection would surface and embarrass me all over again. Thankfully, those instances were few and far between.

"I'm back here now. I was transferred to the Vegas team several weeks ago."

"Are you happy about the change?" she asked, standing beside him with her arm slung over his shoulder.

Granted, they'd been friends as well before he up and left, so the familiarity she projected toward him wasn't unusual. But her being so close to him, all chummy and borderline giddy, bothered me.

"I am. One of my buddies got transferred with me, so that's good. And I'm getting more money. No complaints there, either."

"Good thing, because I read that you're broke," she teased, because one thing Luke wasn't was broke.

I only knew because of my father, who'd followed Luke's entire career, and loved to share information about the guy. He mentioned years ago how he signed a five-year contract for thirty million. And if Luke said he was now making more, I couldn't even imagine what they were paying him. He was one of the best players in the sport, so I was sure he was worth it, but among a hundred other things, I'd never tell him that either.

When Brooke finally returned to her seat, she repeated her original question, the one that made me cringe initially because it meant one of us was going to answer. And if he did, there was no telling how he'd spin it.

"What were you telling him no for when I came back?"

She inched forward so she could see both of us, her attention bouncing from him to me and back again while she waited for one of us to respond.

I decided on: "I don't remember."

Unfortunately, as I suspected, Luke had a different rebuttal.

"I offered to help Ollie here with her issue."

"Ollie." Brooke laughed. "You hated when he called you that."

"I remember." I moved toward her because he was closer to me now than he was a second ago.

"Wait. Go back. You offered to help her with *what* issue?" The inflection in Brooke's voice told me she knew exactly what issue he referred to.

I'd been taking a sip of my drink when he spoke again.

"To help her come during sex."

If he'd phrased his answer any other way, my wine wouldn't have ended up on the ledge of the bar, on my hand, or on my best friend's forearm.

"Damn, woman." She grabbed a napkin and wiped off what I'd spit on her. But she wasn't angry. In fact, when I glanced over at her, she wiggled her brows and had the biggest smile plastered on her face. "I think that's a great idea."

"I don't."

"Why?"

"Before Ollie answers, let me plead my case, if you will."

He was talking to Brooke, of course, because he wasn't going to get anywhere with me. Tactics. It was all tactics. If he could get my best friend to come over to his side, he'd have an ally to help him.

"I can't wait to hear this," she said, rubbing her hands together in eagerness.

I was going to say "me too" but decided against it at the last second.

"I overheard—"

"Eavesdropped," I corrected, crossing my arms over my chest. Which wasn't the best move because I ended up pushing my breasts higher, the slight cleavage I was already sporting now amplified. His gaze veered to my chest before he turned his attention back to Brooke.

"As I was saying." He paused for effect. "I overheard her tell you she wants someone who isn't a psycho. Check. Someone who's attractive, which I believe I am. I mean, people aren't running away scared when they see me, so I think I fit the bill there. Check." He was fully aware of how good-looking he was, and if he didn't, the table of women staring at him was a telltale sign. "She also wants someone to know how to use what they have." He talked like I wasn't sitting right next to him. "I'm not bragging but I have an above-average penis, and I know what to do with it." His use of the word penis and the way he spoke was purposefully clinical like. He either mocked me or placated Brooke. Or perhaps he was just being funny. Whatever it was he was doing, I wasn't amused. "So, check for that one. And as for the last item on the list—"

"That was it. You already covered the requirements," I rushed to say. I didn't want him to mention the last one because I would be bombarded with memories of the two of us in his bedroom, doing what it was he was going to list as the last item.

"No, there was one more," Brooke said. "Go ahead, Luke." She had the audacity to smirk at me when she caught my eye.

"Last requirement," he said, looking at his hand as if he was reading off a piece of paper. "She wants said man to be a good kisser." I couldn't believe he remembered everything I'd told her, listing them in the same order too. "She can already attest that I am." Luke finally turned his head to look at me, but I refused to meet his eyes. "Can't you?"

"You guys kissed? When?" Brooke never waited for an answer when she fired more questions at me. "Why didn't you tell me? You tell me everything else, right?" I hated the suspicion in her voice, but I wasn't about to sit here, in front of him, and dive into why I never told her about the one time we made out.

"Because I wanted to forget it ever happened." Finally lifting my eyes to his, I said, "Besides, I've had better."

"Liar." His response was immediate, arrogant, and right on the money.

"I think you should do it, Liv. Take Luke home and put him to the test. If you want, I can oversee it. Make sure he's doing what he needs to."

"I think I'm capable of handling my business, but thanks for the offer," Luke said.

"If you change your mind, I'm here."

"I assure you—"

"STOP! Enough already. I'm not having sex with Luke."

"Why?" she asked

"Yeah, why?" he parroted.

I placed my feet on the ground and straightened my dress, fiddling with the belt cinched around my waist. "Because I don't like him." My focus was on my friend before I swung my attention to the man beside me, to reiterate my statement. "I don't like you. In fact, I can't stand you."

An indescribable emotion flashed behind his eyes. "That's a strong sentiment."

"I'm aware," I responded, fidgeting where I stood. This conversation was going nowhere fast, and the longer he looked at me, the more I wanted to disappear.

He licked his lips and swallowed, his eyes narrowing slightly before he tossed up what I could only describe as a mask. "There you go. That's perfect. Angry sex or can't-stand-you sex is sometimes the best kind. I'm sure it's exactly what will do the trick. No attachments. No expectations. Other than me making you come so hard you'll forget your name." The intensity in his voice made my stomach flip. "But you won't forget mine."

"Goddamn, Luke." Brooke fanned herself. "You almost make me want to switch teams."

"We *do* have a good team."

She nudged my arm. "This is what you said you wanted. Time to step up and make it happen. You're not going to find anyone better. And he's absolutely right, angry sex can be really fun."

I looked from my best friend to the guy who once broke my heart, weighing the pros and cons. My cons list filled up fast, but the one pro I mentally listed unfortunately outweighed the other side.

And the single item was that I'd finally get to sleep with Luke Sorenson.

"I can't believe I'm even considering this." The deal was

already signed, sealed, and delivered in my head, but I pretended I was still contemplating. Locking eyes with him, I steeled my expression and pointed in his face. "You get one shot. That's it. And we do this tonight."

His only response was an ear-splitting grin.

3

LUKE

AND TO THINK I WAS GOING TO STAY IN AND REST. MY BODY HAD been put through the wringer this past week with constant training and practices, and all I wanted to do was sleep, but something had spurred me to come out tonight.

I'd contemplated going somewhere else but, in the end, McConley's was the best choice. It was a hole in the wall, someplace I wouldn't be continuously hounded for autographs and pictures, or at least that was what I thought. Fame was now part of the deal, but sometimes getting recognized sucked. All I wanted to do was play soccer. I happened to be great at it, hence the money and fame.

After being approached by some fans when I first walked in, I'd been sitting in the far corner of the bar when I noticed Olivia. At first, I thought I was hallucinating. I did a double take, but sure enough, it was her. At some point, I figured I'd run into her, but I didn't think it would be this soon after moving back to Vegas.

To be honest, I was worried about this very scenario because the last time I saw her, our situation was far from ideal. But there was no way she was still angry at me. What happened between us was a decade ago. Although, the woman never left my thoughts for long, so if I continued to think about her, I might've still run through her mind over the years, just not in the same way, I was sure.

For ten minutes I watched her from afar, mesmerized by her slightest of movements. The way she tossed her hair over her shoulder, the auburn color darker than I remembered, exposing her slender neck. The way she threw her head back and laughed at something Brooke said, an action which made me smile, even though the expression was involuntary. I didn't even realize I was doing it until my cheek muscles started to ache. But when she glanced around the bar before leaning into her best friend, I knew whatever she was set to divulge had to be good.

Curiosity prodded me to change seats.

I'd accidentally bumped into her, almost spilling her drink. Luckily, the element of surprise hadn't been lost as she never turned to see who the clumsy ass was who banged into her.

And good thing because I got an earful.

It didn't take me long to figure out what she was talking about, her matter-of-fact points making me rock hard. Thank God for the shelter of the bar's overhang because I adjusted myself three times before I offered her my services.

Which brought us here.

"You get one shot. That's it. And we do this tonight." The look on Olivia's face was a blend of irritation, intrigue, and stubbornness, a heady concoction that once again made my dick twitch against the seam of my jeans.

The bartender, whose name I learned earlier was Hale, approached, interrupting my response to a sentence I never expected to hear.

"You want another?"

"Nah." I swallowed the rest of my drink and pushed the glass toward him. "I'm good."

He jerked his chin toward the group of women seated at the

table near the door, the same ones who approached me while I was talking to Olivia. "Looks like they want more of you."

Olivia turned her head to see who Hale was talking about. When she looked back at me with those beautiful green eyes, she made a noise with her throat, but she didn't say anything. I prayed she didn't back out because what I had planned for her tonight, I'd been thinking about for years.

"Not interested," I finally managed to say.

"Oh, to be you, Sorenson. What a dream it would be."

"I don't have any complaints." I looked at the woman next to me when I uttered the next thought that popped into my head. "And neither will you."

"We'll see."

She turned to face Brooke. Whether she mouthed something to her friend or made a face, I'd never know. But I did steal the opportunity to ogle her.

The green floral dress she wore was snug in all the right places, accentuating her plump backside. And although Olivia wasn't tall, possibly standing around five foot five, give or take an inch, the heels she wore made her legs look like they went on for miles. Okay, maybe not miles. Yards? Yeah, that's a better analogy. Either way, I couldn't wait for her to wrap them around me as I moved inside her.

There went the big guy again, begging to be freed.

We needed to leave before she changed her mind. I leaned in close to make sure she could hear me, the chatter in the bar picking up.

"You ready?"

She answered without looking at me. "Let's go." She hugged her friend before walking toward the door, flinging her purse over her shoulder in what I could only assume was frustration.

"Take care of her," Brooke said, pressing her lips to my cheek afterward.

"I'll do my best." I was two steps away when I turned back. "Are you good to get home?"

"Aren't you sweet." She looked at me like I was crazy for asking the question, though. "I'm good. I'll grab an Uber. Now go do your job." Her laughter trailed behind me while I searched for Olivia.

She was halfway out the door when I caught up with her. *Damn, she's fast.* I reached for her hand, but she pulled her arm away the second my fingers brushed against hers. I chuckled but I doubted she heard me.

This is going to be fun.

4

OLIVIA

As soon as we stepped outside, I welcomed the briskness of the night air, hoping to cool off. But the opposite happened, and I was all too aware why my body's temperature continued to rise. It had everything to do with the man falling into step beside me, even though I didn't want to admit that to myself.

"Do you want to go to my place or yours?"

While I contemplated the answer to his question, I again dodged his hand reaching for mine for the second time. Touching him right now would kick me off my game, as if I had any to begin with. I'd have to allow him to touch me at some point tonight, but holding hands was too intimate for me to handle. The sentiment might sound off base, but it made sense in my head. For now, at least.

"You already have a place? Didn't you just move back?"

"I'm renting until I find a house I want to buy."

My hurried steps took me farther down the sidewalk, but I had no idea where I was going. And neither did he, as was prevalent when he grabbed my arm to stop me.

"What?" I asked when he spun me around and stepped into my

personal space. Craning my neck to look up at him disoriented me. His breath fanned my face, his lips only several inches from mine. Instantly, I was assaulted with the memory of our mouths fused together, as if it was only yesterday when it happened. I'd lied before when I told him I'd been kissed by guys who'd been better than him. He'd called me out and I didn't tell him he was right. No one had made me feel the way he had. He'd essentially ruined me, which was yet another reason for me not to like him.

"I'm happy to walk for miles with you, but we should figure out where it is we're going." He finally took a step back. "My place or yours?"

This time I answered. "Neither. It's only one time, so I say we go to a hotel."

He contemplated my suggestion, making a clicking sound with his mouth as his left eyebrow rose.

"Okay. You win. Hotel it is." He pulled out his phone, typed in something and scrolled. "There's one two blocks down that way." He pointed east of where we stood. "My car is over there," he said, gesturing back toward the bar. "I can drive."

"I'd rather walk." I needed the fresh air to clear my head enough to figure out if I should even be doing this. I agreed Luke was probably the best choice for me to "experiment" with. But when I'd revealed my plan to Brooke, I envisioned a stranger. Someone who, if they judged me afterward, I wouldn't care because I'd never have to see him again. And while this was going to be a one-shot deal tonight, chances were pretty good I'd run into Luke again at some point.

We walked together in silence. My thoughts were jumbled and incomplete. I could only imagine what he was thinking, but there was no way I was going to ask. Something told me I'd regret it.

"Ollie." Luke grabbed my wrist and pulled me back a step.

"What?" I swung my arm back and he let me go.

"We're here. You were going to keep on walking had I not stopped you."

"I saw the hotel," I lied. I brushed past him toward the walkway to the main entrance. "And why do you insist on calling me that?"

"Ollie?" I glanced back at him without answering. "Because it gets under your skin. And it seems only fair." He fell in step with me once again, opening the door for me before I could wrap my fingers around the handle.

"What's only fair?"

"That I get under your skin. Because you got under mine years ago." I refused to dissect his comment, my heels click-clacking across the marble tile, quieting only when I hit a patch of carpet. Before he headed toward the woman standing behind the desk, he may have mumbled, "You're still there" but I couldn't be a hundred percent sure.

As I waited for him to check us in, I tried not to let my nerves get the better of me. I'd fantasized about having sex with him countless times when I was younger, and the one time I offered myself to him, he rejected me. For some reason, I still harbored a piece of the insecurity he'd helped to create, and conjuring the memory angered me all over again.

Maybe he was right.

Angry sex could be the key.

I supposed we'd find out together.

Staring at the back of him, I allowed myself a private moment to appreciate his physique. His black T-shirt was molded to his broad shoulders and toned arms, but looser toward his tapered waist. His dark jeans hung on his hips in a way that made me want to imagine shimmying them down his legs, legs I knew for a fact were muscular from the various pictures plastered on the Internet from one of his many games.

"You ready?" He was suddenly in front of me. I flinched at the sound of his voice because I'd been lost inside my head.

"I have to use the ladies' room," I countered, ignoring the look on his face, which silently screamed "what the hell is wrong with you."

"I'm pretty sure there's a bathroom in the room. Come on." He placed his hand on the small of my back, the heat from his touch disorienting me. What would happen when he put his hands on my naked skin?

"I'll use the one down here." My tone was curt, and I was positive my mouth had turned down in a scowl. But neither fazed him. All he did was roll his eyes and lean against the nearest wall, shoving his hands in his pockets as if he didn't have a care in the world.

Wasn't he the least bit nervous?

Was he really that presumptuous about his abilities in the bedroom?

The restroom was empty, which was a blessing as the words poured from my mouth as soon as the door closed behind me, all my insecurities and doubts bouncing off the walls.

"This is stupid," I mumbled, looking in the mirror. "You're gonna get up to the room and freeze. I can't have sex with him. With Luke Sorenson. I should've picked someone else, a stranger. Someone I don't have any kind of history with. What was I thinking?" My breaths came short and quick, sounding more like a woman in labor than someone who was about to have sex.

After rinsing my mouth with water and checking to make sure my makeup wasn't smudged, I worked to calm my erratic heartbeat before exiting the restroom. But when I saw Luke in the same exact position, another bout of nerves stole over me.

Not a word was spoken during the short walk to the elevator. He pressed the button and we stood side by side waiting for the car to arrive, his hand brushing against mine when he shifted his weight. The chime sounded right before the doors opened and I flinched, even though I'd been expecting it.

"Jumpy?"

I ignored him, stepping inside, and moving to the far-right corner. I half expected him to crowd me, but he stayed near the entrance, giving me my space.

Traveling to the fourth floor should've been quick, but every second inside with him, slowed down time. Time I didn't want because I lost myself to my inner ramblings, yet again.

Once we stepped into the hallway, he tapped the room's key card against his palm, leading me around the corner and to the second door on the right. The click of the lock echoed in the otherwise quiet space.

"What do you think?" he asked, pushing open the door and gesturing for me to enter. A millisecond of hesitation passed through me before I took the first step over the threshold.

"About the room?"

"Yeah. Not bad for last minute."

"It looks clean and has a bed. It'll do."

He waltzed past me and toward the window, drawing the drapes open briefly to look outside. A moment later, he swiveled back around, his gaze landing on mine.

"Were you checking out my ass?"

"No." I had glanced at his butt while he had his back to me, but I'd never admit it.

"Why are your cheeks red?"

"They are not." I touched my face, and sure enough, the warmth blossomed beneath my fingertips.

While I tried to get my wits under control, he was suddenly in front of me, reaching out to feel the heat of my cheeks. I moved to the side before his hand could connect.

"They are. I think it's cute you're embarrassed you got caught checking me out." He widened his stance and stretched his arms to his sides. "Stare all you want. But I can assure you I look better naked." All I could do was huff in response as he did a dramatically slow turn, winking at me once he was faced forward again.

"Were you always this arrogant?" My question was rhetorical, of course, because he most certainly was. But for some reason, I'd found it charming when I was younger. Now... not so much.

We weren't touching, but the intensity radiating from him was enough to make me want to squirm. But I didn't move a muscle. I didn't want to give him the satisfaction of calling me out again.

Awkward moments of silence bounced between us as we regarded each other. At least it was awkward for me. For him, I couldn't readily tell because that grin was still plastered on his face.

"Can I kiss you now?" he asked, finally slicing through the quiet. His focus was on my mouth, raising his eyes to mine for only a second before he was back to staring at my lips.

Words bubbled up in my throat, but I couldn't give them the air needed to bring them to life. All I could do was stand there, staring back at him. After several deep breaths, I nodded. There was no time like the present to get this started.

The moment he stepped closer, my blood rushed faster, and I wasn't sure if it was because I wanted this to happen or if I dreaded what would happen because of it.

He cradled my face in his hands, tilting until he positioned me how he wanted, his mouth brushing over mine. He pulled away as I leaned into him, and when he came close again, he only hovered.

"Are you going to just tease me?"

"I haven't decided yet." Lowering his hands to my waist, he dug his fingers in, and yanked me forward, his mouth covering mine. His lips were soft yet firm, and he tasted of mint and scotch. The first slide of his tongue made me dizzy, the second intensified the ache between my legs. All my senses went into overdrive, but before I could enjoy his kiss, he severed the connection and retreated several steps, his eyes pinned to mine the entire time.

Without saying a word, he bunched the neck of his shirt and pulled it over his head, tossing it on a nearby chair.

He had the most amazing chest, all sinewy and chiseled. I could spend forever staring at those sculpted abs of his. But my favorite part of his physique were his arms. They were perfect. Not too muscular, just the right amount of bulk and tone.

Instead of giving him a compliment, however, all I said was "I can work with that."

He licked his lips in response. "Now let me see what I'll be working with."

I realized since we were going to be having sex, I'd have to get naked. But standing in front of him, still clothed, with him waiting for me to disrobe, my stomach did a few somersaults.

Resting my fingers on the belt of my wrap dress, I tugged the one side, but not enough to unravel the tie. "If I take this off, I'll only have my bra and underwear on." I waved my finger up and down his body. "You'll still be half dressed."

Was I trying to buy more time? Absolutely.

Would it work? I hoped so.

He was silent as he kicked off his shoes, pulled off his socks, and popped the button of his jeans. The corner of his mouth curved upward when he slowly dragged the zipper down through its teeth, the sound reverberating in the small space. When his fingers disappeared beneath the waistband, he shimmied both his jeans and underwear down his legs, his thick arousal pointing directly at me when he stood back up to his full height of six one.

I didn't want to stare, but I was powerless to stop myself. His body was perfection, so much so he made me feel much more self-conscious. His skin was a gorgeous shade of golden brown, and because I didn't see any visible tan lines, I wanted to ask him if he sunbathed nude, but I didn't utter the words, too enraptured with soaking him all in.

His fingers locked around his shaft, tossing me out of my own head. "Can you work with this?"

He wasn't lying when he said he was above average. No wonder the guy was so cocky, all puns intended. Again, I didn't stroke his ego. Although, I was sure he wanted me to stroke something else.

I lifted my shoulder in a half shrug. "It'll do, I guess."

His eyes narrowed and I waited for him to say something, to call me out, to make me compliment him. Something. But he simply continued to stare at me, reveling in the silence that followed, his expression one of expectation.

"Come on, Ollie. I showed you mine. Now it's your turn. Take off your clothes." There was a time all I dreamt about was hearing such a thing tumble from his mouth, and while they thrilled me now, I wasn't the same person I was ten years ago. There was a bit of irritation, mainly from the nickname he insisted on using, that swirled with my excitement, forming a whole other emotion altogether. He took a single step toward me, and I held up my hand to stop him. "Do you want me to help you? Because I would have no problem with that."

"No. I don't need your help." He drew a quick glare from me that didn't seem to faze him.

"If you don't want to do this," he said, advancing another stride in my direction, "we don't have to." Why did it irritate me that he gave me the option to change my mind? "But you'll never know if you can come." His bottom lip disappeared between his teeth before popping free. "During sex, I mean."

"I know what you meant." I blew out a breath. "I don't want out, and I don't need your help to get undressed. I just need a minute."

"Why?"

"Because I'm not sure I can follow that," I said, gesturing up and down his incredible body. "I mean, come on. It's like you've used some kind of filter on yourself."

"I assure you everything about me is real. Wanna touch?" I said, "No," and nodded at the same time. When I didn't make a move to undress, he said, "If you don't get naked, we can't get on with it. So, what do you say?"

Numerous responses rattled through my overactive brain, but when I finally settled on one, a surge of courage churned inside me.

"All right. I'll take off my dress."

"And the rest of it."

"I'll take off everything. But I'm warning you now, my chest is small, and my butt is big, so if you make any derogatory comments about either, I'm leaving." For as confident as I wanted to appear, I couldn't stop the tremble in my hands as I separated the fabric belt that held my dress together.

"Lucky for you, I'm an ass man." When I didn't say anything in response, his eyes softened. "I would never say anything negative. In fact, any guy who did should be kicked in the balls. I know you think I'm going to judge you, but trust me, the second I see you naked, it's going to take every ounce of my self-control not to pounce on you. I bet you're perfect. In fact, I'd stake my life on it."

His words helped to ease some of my anxiety. When the sides of my dress parted, I pushed the material off my shoulders, and I was left standing there in my purple bra and my white, polka-dotted panties. Had I known the night would lead to sex with Luke, I would've worn a matching set. But obviously, I could've never predicted such an occurrence.

Deciding it was best to get this over with, I reached behind my back and unhooked my bra, tossing it to the floor as soon as the cups had fallen. Seconds later, I hurriedly pulled down my underwear, kicking them to the side.

With my head down and my eyes now closed, I counted my

shallow breaths. I wanted to cover my breasts, but I didn't want to let him know the level of my insecurity, so I kept my arms at my sides.

"See? I knew you'd be perfect."

My eyes snapped open, and for the first time since I laid eyes on him tonight, a genuine smile caressed my lips.

5

LUKE

LIKE I KNEW SHE WOULD BE, SHE WAS PERFECT. AND THERE WAS something about the timid way she stood before me that turned me on even more. I wanted to touch every inch of her, reassuring her I loved each part, because I did.

I'd imagined her body more times than I could count over the years, but this was the first time I'd ever seen her naked. I'd seen her in a bikini when we were younger, so I had an idea of what she looked like. Her body had changed over the years, though, and while her chest was a similar size, her hips had filled out. Her ass had also gotten bigger from when she was a teenager, and I was dying to turn her around to see the real deal.

For as much as I wanted to wrap my lips around her hardened, pink nipples, my mouth watering at the sight, this wasn't about me. It was all about her. I needed to find out what she liked and what she didn't.

I closed the small gap between us, towering over her. Her breasts pressed against me as I raised her head. Tenderly, I covered her mouth with mine, but I didn't deepen the kiss. We needed to have a little chat first.

"Is there anything you don't like to do?"

Her breath fanned my lips, and for a moment I thought she was going to ignore my question. "I've never tried it, but I don't want to do anal."

I couldn't help the bubble of laughter that erupted from me. "I doubted that was on the table anyway. But it might be the key," I teased.

"Pass."

Moving my hands to her waist, I walked her backward, and all I wanted to do was throw her down and bury myself inside her, but again, I refrained, albeit barely.

"What's your favorite position?"

Her eyes shifted downward, then sideways before she looked back up at me. "I like missionary. I know it's boring, but I like the feeling of the guy on top of me."

"Okay. Are you open to other positions as well?"

"Sure."

Standing so close, I could feel the heat of her body, the slight tremble of her muscles as she pretended she wasn't as affected as I was with the proximity.

"You know you can touch me if you want."

"I know," she responded, lifting her right hand only to place it on my waist. I was hoping she'd go lower, but I'd let her go at her own pace.

"Is there anything else you don't want to do?"

"I can't think of anything right now."

"Is there anything a guy has done that you've liked?"

"Of course." Her hand fell away, and she stepped back, but she couldn't go far because the wall was right behind her. My question somehow annoyed her, but I didn't know why. "I'm not some robot who doesn't feel pleasure during sex." Her cheeks flushed. "It's just that I can't orgasm."

"I didn't think that at all. I'm only trying to figure out where to start off. I want to make this experience as pleasurable as possible for you, with one goal in mind."

Allowing a moment to pass before I asked another question proved to be helpful. "Do you like it when a guy goes down on you?" The image of another man getting to taste her irked me. The feeling was irrational, but it spiraled through me just the same.

"I don't know."

"What do you mean, you don't know? You've never had a guy go downtown?"

"Downtown? Really?" She tilted her head before shaking it.

"Answer the question."

"Yes, I've had boyfriends go down on me, but it's never for long. After a few..." She swallowed her next words, shifting from one foot to the other. "They didn't like it, I guess."

"What guy doesn't like eating pussy?"

She never answered. But I didn't expect her to.

Deciding talk time was over, I snatched her hands and raised them above her head, holding them both in one of mine, pinning her between me and the wall.

"If at any time you want to stop, or try something else, just tell me. Okay? No faking anything, and no going along because you think it's what I want. You're in complete control. I'm only here to service you."

A nod was her only response.

With my free hand, I gripped her jaw, moving my thumb toward her mouth. I licked at the seam of her lips, and as she parted them, I dipped my thumb inside, just enough to tease us both. She closed her mouth and sucked the tip. When I moved back, keeping her hands captive above her, she groaned, which made me happy. She didn't dislike me as much as she pretended to. Or if she did, her feelings toward me didn't stop her from wanting me.

Snaking my arm around her, I gripped her ass. In desperate need to see it, I released her and turned her around so quickly, she had to lay her hands on the wall to keep from falling.

"What are you—"

I was on my knees before she finished her question, reveling in the gloriousness of her plump backside. I hadn't lied when I told her I was an ass man, and she had the best one I'd ever seen. It was bitable, spankable, and fuckable, although anal sex was off the table. Not that I would do that with her the first time anyway.

There's only going to be this one time.

Disappointment ricocheted inside me, but I didn't want to waste any mental energy on the thought. I needed to focus. Hell, it was hard not to, with all of this in front of my face.

I pinched her cheek right before I bared my teeth and bit her. Not hard, but enough to have her pushing back into me.

"Spread your legs. Wider." With one hand, I grasped her waist, and with the other, I pushed on the middle of her back until she was leaning over but still able to brace herself against the wall. I wanted to say so many things. Dirty things. Questionable things. But I never uttered a word as I spread her cheeks, dipped lower, and ran my tongue over her wet center. She bucked against me, groaning at the contact. I did it again, this time using my fingers to spread her excitement.

For the next several minutes I licked, sucked, and nibbled at her like she was my last meal, and until this moment I hadn't realized how hungry I'd been.

Olivia had made many an appearance as I'd pleasured myself over the years, but the reality of her was so much better.

She seemed to be enjoying herself, but because I couldn't see her face, I wasn't sure. I'd told her not to fake anything, but there was a possibility she'd gone against my wishes.

Without warning, I pulled away, even though I hated to, and stood up. My abrupt departure had her spinning around, saying something that made me want to snatch the words from the air and crush them in my fist.

"See? Guys don't like it. Or they don't like doing it to me." A sexy shade of pink rose over her throat and exploded on her cheeks.

I seized her hand and pulled her toward the queen-size bed before she could wallow in any more self-doubt.

"I'm not stopping. I want you on your back. I need to see your face. And in case there's any confusion, I love burying my tongue between your legs."

She sucked in a breath, and I could see the excitement swirl behind her eyes, even though she tried to mask her stare with indifference.

Olivia Brighton was crumbling right in front of me, and there wasn't a damn thing she could do to stop it.

I'd make sure of it.

6

OLIVIA

Luke looked to a spot on the bed, and I situated myself there. When he stared at my legs, which were pinned together, and crooked his brow, the muscles in his jaw ticked when I didn't spread them quick enough.

There was something to this nonverbal communication. I liked it, especially since I didn't know what was going to come flying out of his mouth. He could turn me on one second, and piss me off in the next.

There was a time when I believed I was in love with him, but after what he did, my infatuation toward him turned from hurt to anger. I told him I couldn't stand him earlier, but that was only half true, which would be the explanation needed for why I was so turned on by him right now.

"You're so beautiful," he said, lowering himself on top of me, nestling his hips over mine while he rested on his forearms to hold most of his weight off me. "I bet you have guys falling at your feet, don't you?"

"Not quite." I didn't mean for my tone to take on such a harsh edge. Or did I?

"I think you're being modest. When was the last time a guy hit on you?"

"Tonight."

"Funny. Besides me."

I sighed. "I suppose it was when I met my ex."

"How long ago was that?" He shifted his weight, and the tip of his arousal slid against my sex, and for a moment I lost my train of thought.

"A year and a half."

"What happened with him? Why did you break up?" His lips rested against my throat, the rumble of his voice when he spoke sending a chill through my entire body.

"I don't want to talk about it."

"Okay."

Suddenly he leaned back on his haunches, staring down at me, his focus traveling from my face to my breasts to between my legs.

"What are you doing?" I fought the urge to cover myself, the intensity of his stare suddenly making it hard to breathe or form a coherent thought.

"I'm getting prepared." He stretched his neck from side to side, placed his right hand over his left fist, cracked his knuckles and did the same for his opposite hand. "I want you to know I'm not going to half-ass this. I'll give it my all. I promise you."

"I think you might be taking this a little too seriously." What I wanted to tell him was that I appreciated his effort so far and had no doubt he'd give this task his all. But again, I kept my thoughts to myself, needing my guard in place where he was concerned. As much as possible, given our current situation, of course.

"Orgasms are serious business." The glint in his eye was the only sign he was having fun with me right now. "What do you want to do first?"

There was no hesitation on my part when I answered. "I liked what you were doing before."

"Good. So did I."

When he moved his face toward mine, I thought he was going to kiss me, but he only brushed his mouth over mine before moving toward my breasts. The scruff of his beard skated over my hardened nipple, and I sucked in a lungful of air. They'd always been sensitive, too sensitive sometimes.

He circled the peak with the tip of his tongue, closed his lips around it, and sucked gently before applying the softest pressure with his teeth. He moved to tease the other, lavishing his attention between them as he kneaded my breasts. The popping noise his mouth made when he released one of my nipples sounded amplified.

"Do you like what I'm doing?"

I nodded.

"Do you want me to go farther south?"

Again, I nodded.

He moved so quickly, if I hadn't been paying attention, he would've startled me. With his hands on each of my legs, he spread me wide, trailing kisses along my inner thighs. He'd get close to where I wanted him to be, then move away at the last second. The third time he did it, I grabbed his hair and pulled.

His eyes veered toward mine. "Stop teasing me. We don't have all night."

"Ah, but we do."

I couldn't argue because it wasn't really that late, and I didn't have to be at work until ten tomorrow, although he didn't know my schedule.

Luke was the first guy in a long time who enjoyed going down on me, and I was anxious to see if this could be the thing that would help me.

"Please." On our way over here, I promised myself that no

matter what I wasn't going to beg him for anything, but I was in a situation now that called for a bit of pleading.

"Say it again." He flattened his tongue and ran it over the length of me.

I tangled more of his hair between my fingers and yanked harder than before.

"Please," I repeated, just as he'd instructed.

"I like hearing you beg. I'm going to have to make sure you do it more often."

I didn't have a response, too focused on how he flicked his tongue over my clit, switching from slow to fast and back again.

When he pushed two fingers inside me, I arched my back before thrusting toward his mouth. "That feels...." My breath escaped my lungs in a rush, the rest of whatever I was going to say evaporating completely.

"Do you like it better when I do this?" He sucked hard on the most sensitive part of me. "Or this?" He licked the entire length of me while pumping his fingers into me, pressing his thumb over the bundle of nerves afterward. "Or all of it?"

"All of it." I teetered between pushing him away and pulling him closer. The sensations were too much. What he was doing felt amazing, but unfortunately, not enough to make me climax. After another ten minutes, I tapped on his shoulders. "It's not going to happen that way. Can we try something else?"

"Are you sure? I can do this for as long as you want." He stretched his mouth and massaged along his jawline.

"Looks to me like your mouth is sore."

"I'll be good to go in one minute." He continued to move his jaw from side to side, rubbing at the muscles.

"That's okay. I'd like to have sex now."

In all the time I'd spent in relationships, I'd never been as comfortable sexually with any of them as I was with Luke. At the time, I'd loved whoever I was with, but in hindsight there had always been something missing.

But with Luke, I didn't quite know how to put my finger on it. Was it because I didn't love him? That I still harbored anger toward him? Was that the difference?

Granted, there'd been moments when we first shed our clothes that I'd been a tad unsure or anxious or whatever the feeling was. But now, all I wanted was to instruct him on what to do. Or listen to him give me multiple choice questions relating to oral sex.

"If you're gonna twist my arm." He playfully smacked my thigh before hopping off the bed, striding across the room, his gait confident, sexy. I stole the opportunity to stare at his butt. It really was a work of art. "You're staring at my ass again."

"So?"

"I don't mind." He rooted through the pockets of his jeans "Shit."

"What's wrong?"

"I thought I had a condom in my wallet, but I don't." He turned partway to glance at me.

"What's that look for?" I asked.

"Are you on the pill or any type of birth control?"

"Why?"

"Because unless you have a condom in your purse, we don't have one."

I sat up in bed, loving the way his eyes scoured over my bare breasts. "I guess we're done." My voice belied my inner turmoil. What I said was so matter of fact, but inside I was punching the mattress and screaming, *Why did this have to happen now?*

"Unless...," Luke dragged out the word.

"Unless what?" Realization dawned on me, and I filled in the blank before he had the opportunity to answer. "I'm not sleeping with you without a condom. God only knows how many women you've been with. I'm not catching something because you want to raw dog it."

"Raw dog it? Oh, Lord." He shook his head and smiled. "Sounds like something I would say, not you."

"You don't own the market on stupid slang phrases."

He ignored my retort, rifling through his pocket again, this time to pull out his cell. He was busy typing, and scrolling, repeating the action for a full minute before speaking again.

"First off, I've always used a condom before, and contrary to what you might believe, my number of sexual partners probably isn't as high as you think. Secondly, how do I know you don't have something? I'm sure you get around."

"How dare—"

He looked up from his phone. "Sorry. That came out wrong. It's not what I meant. The getting around part. You're gorgeous and I'm sure you've had your opportunities to sleep with whomever you wanted. No shame."

"If you must know, I've only been with three guys. All of whom I was in a relationship with. And as far as having a disease, I can assure you I don't. After I caught my ex cheating, I got tested." Just speaking about what happened angered me. "I have a clean bill of health."

"What an asshole."

"He was."

Luke focused on me for several seconds but didn't say anything. I couldn't tell by his expression what he was thinking. Was he pitying me?

When I shifted on the bed, his attention swung back to the device in his hand.

"What are you looking at?"

He walked toward the bed and sat on the edge, inches from me. "We have to get a physical once a year, and mine was two weeks ago." He turned his phone toward me so I could see. "I got a clean bill of health too. And I haven't slept with anyone since."

"A whole two weeks? However did you survive?" I snatched

the phone from him and scrolled, reading the medical jargon. Sure enough, his results were negative for all the diseases they tested for, which were extensive. "Is this something you do? Access this to show women so you don't have to wear a condom?"

"I told you. I've always worn a condom. And you're the only person to see this, besides my coach."

I stared at the screen longer than necessary, wondering whether to forgo the latex barrier.

"You never answered me before. Are you on the pill?"

"Yes."

"Good. That means we can raw dog it tonight." The corners of his eyes crinkled when he repeated the slang phrase.

We were both healthy, and I *was* on the pill. After a moment of biting my lip in contemplation, I handed him back his phone.

"Okay."

"Okay?"

"That's what I said."

The smile that lit up his face was contagious. I tried to fight my grin but lost the battle.

He tossed his phone on the bedside table and moved toward me with a hungry look in his eyes, a stare that made me ache with the need to give him anything he wanted.

"I've imagined this so many times, you have no idea," he said, positioning himself over me, spreading my legs so he could nestle in between.

Instead of lashing out at him, screaming that he could've had me years ago but didn't want me, I harnessed the anger and allowed it to coil deep in my belly.

"I'm already wet. I don't need any more foreplay," I grumbled when he kissed the column of my throat and played with my nipple.

"What if I do?" He sucked at my neck. "I don't want to rush

this." His hand traveled from my nipple to my waist, moving lower until his fingers danced over my core.

"Luke." I said his name in warning, harsh and demanding.

He never stopped stroking me. "I thought you liked this."

"I do."

"What's the problem?"

I wanted to shout at him that *he* was the problem. He'd made me angry when he said what he did, dredging up old feelings of embarrassment and heartache. After several long moments of internal deliberation, however, all I uttered was one word.

"Nothing."

"No, there's something wrong." He removed his hand from between my legs and rested it on my hip bone, his eyes boring into me like he was trying to read my mind.

"I just want to have sex."

"Is that it? There's nothing else on your mind? Something you want to talk about?"

"What is this? Therapy? I thought we were going to fuck, not get all mushy." I had no idea any of those words were going to come flying out of my mouth until they did. I supposed the anger I'd tried to suppress didn't stay hidden long enough.

His chest expanded on an inhale, and his expression leveled right before his mouth crashed over mine. He plunged his tongue inside, his aggressiveness a result of my words, and he was giving me what I'd asked for. So why did a small piece of me long for his tender side?

Luke severed the kiss, his eyes dark and foreboding as he lifted himself onto his forearms, positioned himself at my entrance, and worked himself inside me on a stifled moan, thrusting as deep as he could and holding himself there. His head snapped back, the noise that bubbled up his throat spurring my excitement to new heights, navigating me through the bite of pain from my muscles being stretched around the girth of him.

When his head finally dropped, and his eyes landed on mine, he circled his hips, the movement precise, deliberate. An unfamiliar tingle traveled through me and I held my breath, waiting for the next wave, but when he rotated his hips again, the sensation eluded me.

"You're so wet," he panted. "And tight. I don't want to move too fast, but I also want to fuck you so hard your throat will be raw from screaming."

"Confident, aren't you?" My unexpected teasing tone pleased him.

"I am." Withdrawing until only the tip remained, he sank back in, smooth and steady, the torment of his body the sweetest I'd ever experienced. "Does that feel good?" The muscles in his chest rippled with his exertion, his every movement controlled. "I can go faster if you want. Tell me what you like. I'll do anything."

"Go a little faster." I didn't know if it was his size or the way he rocked into me, but I felt something. Not the tingle from before, but... pleasure. I just didn't think it would be enough. Dissuading myself from already calling it quits, I focused on the guy looming over me.

He really was the most beautiful-looking man I'd ever seen, a sentiment I'd keep to myself because I didn't want to inflate his ego. I was sure his millions of adoring fans did that enough. The image of how those women fawned all over him earlier came to mind.

"Am I hurting you?" He stopped moving altogether and pushed himself up, putting more distance between us while remaining inside me.

I hadn't realized I'd made a face, but apparently my thoughts transferred to my expression.

"No, you're not hurting me." We entered a drawn-out staring contest and unfortunately, I lost. Turning my head to the side to evade the look he threw at me, one I couldn't quite decipher yet,

I released the breath in my lungs. But my escape didn't last long at all.

"Olivia. Look at me." The absence of my nickname was what made me comply. "I know you don't particularly like me, but I'd really like to make you come, so stay with me here. Please." He kissed me tenderly as he moved once more, going deeper than before.

"Wrap your legs around me. Hook your ankles together. Just like that," he whispered in my ear, capturing my lobe with his teeth. "You feel amazing. I love your pussy." He licked the shell of my ear. I groaned. "Do you want it harder?" Luke gripped the headboard above me and thrust deeper, which I didn't think was even feasible. "Tell me you love my cock." He grunted out his last request, the heat from his body igniting mine.

Instead of responding to his demand, I begged, "Keep doing that," and found the tingle once more. I tried to grab on to it, matching his rhythm with my own, but again it was fleeting. "Fuck!"

"Are you close?" His voice was filled with hope, his gyrations increasing the closer he thought I was.

"No. That 'fuck' was in frustration."

"Oh. Well, let's try something else."

And try something else we did indeed.

Luke flipped me around like I weighed nothing at all, putting me into all sorts of positions, more than I'd ever been in before. First, he was on top of me, then I was in his lap. Moments later he was behind me, driving into me while he stroked me with his fingers. At one point, I was hanging half off the bed, dangling upside down. Not that I didn't enjoy it, but I was no closer to climaxing than when we started. It seemed I wouldn't be able to achieve what I set out to do, no matter what we tried. But one thing was for certain. Tonight was the best time I'd ever had. I thoroughly enjoyed the sex, counting the tingling sensations as a win. They were more than I'd ever experienced before with my three ex-boyfriends. Not to mention the way he went down on me. Good Lord. The man knew how to use his tongue.

Thirty-eight minutes later, we were back to missionary, and I decided it was time I called it. He was in the middle of kissing my neck when I tapped his shoulder.

"You want to try something else?" He raised up, the strain of his weight evident in the bulge of his biceps.

"What else could there be?"

"There's more. Or we can make some up." He jerked his hips forward before pulling back, over and over. Quick. Slow. Shallow. Deep. The entire time he kept his eyes on me.

Reaching down, I gripped his waist, essentially making him stop. "It's not going to happen, Luke. You gave it your best, but I can't do it. I can't come. But you can." I smacked his ass. "You can finish."

"No."

"What do you mean, no?"

"If you can't come, I won't either."

"Don't be crazy. I'm shocked you held out this long. It's okay really. I want you to." I widened my legs, gripped his firm backside, and gyrated against him. "Do it. Fuck me hard and come inside me."

"Christ, Ollie. Don't say shit like that."

This was the first time the sound of my nickname didn't irritate me.

"Say what? Fuck me hard? Or come inside me?"

"Both, but more the last one." His lips moved as if he were speaking but he didn't say anything out loud.

"What are you doing?"

"I'm thinking of everything I can that's a turnoff, so I don't explode." His breaths came short and fast as he pulled out and moved beside me.

"Why didn't you finish?"

"I meant what I said. If you don't come, neither do I." After several minutes of him sitting next to me, he turned me on my side, facing away from him, and wrapped his body around me from behind, playing with my nipple as his warm breath fanned my ear.

I tried to move away, but he trapped me in his embrace. When I tried once more, he grunted and threw his leg over mine to keep me right where he wanted me.

"Stop trying to get away from me, woman." My third attempt at escape proved futile, so I huffed out my frustrations and snuggled back into him. If he wouldn't release me, the least I could do was be comfortable. On a sigh, my eyes drifted close. I had no intention of falling asleep, but the rhythmic beat of his heart thudding against my back relaxed me. But my bliss was short-lived when he spoke again, his voice startling me because he'd been quiet for the past few minutes. "I have a proposition for you."

7

LUKE

I WENT INTO THIS CHALLENGE EXCITED I'D FINALLY GET TO SLEEP with the woman who had been in the back of my mind over the years, often at the forefront.

We'd just finished having sex in more positions than I ever had before during a single encounter with anyone, and I wanted more.

More of her body.

More of her kisses.

More of her sass.

More of the way she looked at me with adoration. The glances were infrequent, and only lasted a second, but when I caught one of them, my heart would swell.

I'd failed her tonight, but I'd be damned if I wouldn't keep at it until she was completely satisfied. Call it ego or the need to finish a challenge, but Olivia would be screaming my name at some point. The sentiment was what prompted me to say, "I have a proposition for you."

She pushed her ass back into me, burrowing under my skin the more she allowed me to hold her close. My dick twitched at the tease, and there was nothing I could do to stop it from hardening.

"It's pointless to try again tonight."

"I agree." I loved that she said "tonight." I doubted she realized what door she had just left open. One I was going to walk through without hesitation.

"Good. We're on the same page. No more sex." That damn door almost slammed in my face, but I held it open.

"Not exactly." I kissed her shoulder, fighting the need to position her on all fours and sink back inside her, reveling at the sight of her gorgeous ass as I took her from behind.

"What do you mean?"

"What I mean is I have a proposition for you."

"So you've mentioned."

I moved back so I could roll her over, needing to see her beautiful face when I continued. Her hair fanned around her and the slight flush to her skin screamed she'd been good and truly fucked. Too bad the satiated look was missing. Something I was all too willing to correct if she'd let me.

Drawing circles around her nipples, I wanted to distract her enough she didn't refuse right away. My goal was for her to agree, to see the possibilities of something good if she'd commit to what I was going to offer.

"How about this? I continue to try and make you orgasm during sex. Not tonight, but going forward until it happens. I'd be willing to put in the time and effort because that's how much I care about your needs." She rolled her eyes. I was completely serious, but my words took on a hint of jest.

"Will you continue to not finish unless I do?"

This is good. She hasn't shot me down yet.

"Yes." I trailed my finger over her soft skin, between her breasts to her belly before moving lower, stopping directly above where I wanted to tease. Leaning in, I kissed her softly. "If you don't come, neither will I." She lifted her head off the pillow to deepen the kiss, but I pulled away. I loved her groan of frustration; it meant she could stand me a bit more than she proclaimed she couldn't.

"What's in it for you, besides unfulfilled sex?"

"There's nothing unfulfilled about the sex we had," I corrected. "I didn't come, but it was the most fun I'd ever had. But to get to your question, I need a plus one to my sister's wedding in two months. I want you to go with me. I'll agree to work to satisfy you in bed, and you agree to be my date."

"Heather is getting married?" she asked excitedly.

"Not the point I wanted you to focus on, but yeah." I turned her toward me, both of us now on our sides. "What do you say?"

"Why?"

"I told you why. I need a date."

"You can take anyone. Why me?"

Grabbing a handful of her ass, I pressed my arousal against her belly. "I think it's a fair trade-off, don't you?" I refused to answer her question, believing if I told her exactly what ran through my head, I'd scare her away. My thoughts barely sounded sane to me, there was no way I was going to voice them to her.

"I don't think it's a good idea," she finally said, moving to turn back over, but I held her in place.

"Please."

I wasn't above begging at this point. I really did need a date to Heather's wedding, but more so, I wanted to help Olivia out, and myself in the process. I wasn't going to lie and say that having sex with her continuously was a hardship because it was the opposite. I didn't want to give her up yet. I'd only gotten a taste, and I was hungry for more.

Some of the longest minutes of my life passed until she finally spoke, the pensive look on her face not indicative to how I thought she would answer.

"If we do this," she started, covering my mouth with her

hand when I started to interject, "you won't sleep with anyone else until we're done."

I removed her hand from my mouth. "Deal. And the same goes for you." Her nod was quick, no hesitancy at all.

"I can't believe I agreed to this," she mumbled, removing my hand from her ass, and shifting toward the edge of the bed.

"Where are you going? I changed my mind about having more sex. I thought we could try again."

Olivia glanced down at my hardened state and smirked, shoving at my shoulder until I fell on my back. "Not going to happen tonight. I'm a little sore, and besides, I have to leave. I have work tomorrow." She hopped off the bed before I could stop her.

"I have practice. So what?"

"Sore," she repeated, turning her back on me.

"I told you I was above average."

"Shut up," she said with a laugh. I thought for sure she was going to get dressed, but she waltzed toward the bathroom as if she didn't have a care in the world, different from the woman earlier tonight. When she reemerged, she reached for her clothes, snapping her bra in place before sliding her panties on. I shot off the bed and was next to her before she put on her dress.

"Stay a little longer." I didn't particularly enjoy the pleading tone of my voice, but I didn't want her to leave yet.

"I can't."

Without thinking, I backed her against the nearest wall. "Can we try again tomorrow night?" I asked, swiping my tongue through her mouth, not wanting her to tell me no. She kissed me back with an intensity I hadn't expected, gripping on to my shoulders, and sliding her fingers through my hair to hold me in place. When I slipped my hand beneath the waistband of her panties, she gently shoved me away, touching her lips as if she couldn't believe we just kissed.

"I can't. I have dinner with my parents, which I'm not looking forward to."

"Why?"

Olivia sidestepped me and snatched her dress from the floor, slipping it over her shoulders and pulling the sides together to cinch the fabric belt.

"Because I think my mom is trying to set me up again."

I was so enthralled with watching her that I almost missed what she'd said. When her words registered, a feeling akin to jealousy erupted within me. Scratch that... it was raging jealousy.

"Why?" I parroted, unable to conjure a different question.

"Because she tells me it's time I settle down. I only broke up with Cody four months ago. I need time, but she doesn't understand that, telling me I'm not getting any younger. I'm only twenty-six."

"Twenty-seven in four months," I added, remembering her birthday was only a few weeks from mine.

"Right. Still young, I think."

"If it makes you feel any better, my mom says the same thing to me."

Instead of continuing the idle banter, her eyes scoured over me, lingering first on my mouth, moving lower until she was solely focused on my dick. She sucked in a small breath when it twitched, but I didn't say a word, allowing her as much time as she wanted to gawk at me. Was she remembering the way I felt inside her, the way I bent her into countless positions?

Olivia finally broke the silence when she cleared her throat and walked toward where her shoes were scattered on the floor.

"I have to get going." After she slipped on her heels, she grabbed her purse and headed toward the door. For some reason, it hadn't dawned on me that I had no idea if she'd driven to the bar or had taken an Uber. And if that was the case, there was no way I was going to let her take one home.

"Did you drive?" I was busy getting dressed while I waited for her to answer.

"No." She pulled her cell from her purse and swiped the screen, but I snagged it from her hand. "What are you doing?"

"I'll take you home."

"That's okay."

"I insist." Resting the phone under my chin, I buttoned my jeans, and shoved the device into my back pocket while I pulled my shirt on.

"Seriously, I can get home by myself." Her arm was stretched toward me, her palm up and waiting for me to give her back her phone.

"I know you're fully capable, but I want to take you."

She contemplated my offer. "Fine. Can I have my cell back now?"

"Sure." After exchanging numbers, I handed her back her property. "Do you live close?"

"Same place I've always lived."

"You still live with your parents?" I supposed I could cross her place off the list for our future meetups.

"No. They wanted to downsize, so I bought it from them last year."

Taking one last look around the room to make sure we hadn't forgotten anything, I moved to open the door, but she beat me to it.

"That's a big place just for you."

"I thought I could start my own family someday, but things aren't turning out as I planned." There was a vulnerability in her voice that made me want to hug her, but she stiffened her spine and trudged two steps ahead of me. "All the better. I like being by myself anyway."

Why did my heart sputter when she uttered those words?

8

LUKE

"Sorenson! Where the hell is your head at?" Coach yelled
from across the field, probably sprouting a few more grays
because of me. "That's the third time you missed the cross." My
only response was to jerk my chin toward him, acknowledging
his reprimand. Not that it helped, because five minutes later I
missed a perfect header. The team took their practices seriously,
as they should, and had this been an actual game, Coach
would've benched me.

This wasn't me. I was never this unfocused. And there was
only one thing I could blame it on, or rather, one specific
person.

"What's going on, man?" Ben asked, leaning over, and resting
his hands on his thighs. "You better get it together before you
get pulled from the game next week. You know Coach doesn't
play around with that shit."

He was right. Our coach, Peter Hawkin, was one of the
toughest in the sport. Not only had he been an all-star player in
his day, but he was one of the most tenured coaches in the
league.

"I know." Sweat poured down my face, the midday sun

beating down on me, working to drain me of whatever energy remained. We'd been at it for over three hours, and I didn't doubt for a second that practice would be extended because of me.

"I got a lot on my mind." I lifted the bottom of my shirt to wipe away the exertion.

Ben shot me a disapproving look before he jogged off toward the center of the field, positioning himself close to Tom and Andy, all three of their expressions too similar for my liking.

Tom Collins, a name I laughed at when he first told me because it just so happened to be my mom's favorite drink, and Andy Tynan, had been with the team for four years, and they were the first two to welcome me. The other guys were okay, if a bit standoffish, which I was sure had everything to do with the rumors that I was some sort of hothead or diva type. Nothing could be further from the truth.

I didn't need any of them to give me the side-eye. I knew what was at stake if I didn't get my head out of my ass. We were set to play my former team, the Miami Mavericks, in six days, and I didn't want to negatively impact the possible win because I struggled to keep focus.

For the rest of practice, I tried my hardest to concentrate, burying all thoughts of Olivia as best I could. And even though I accomplished the not-so-easy feat, it didn't stop Coach from reaming me out after practice had finally ended.

After a quick shower, I was getting dressed when Ben appeared next to me with his bag flung over his shoulder. I thought he was on his way out, but he took a seat on the bench in the locker room, staring at me, like I was supposed to know what was on his mind. To be fair, I did.

The last thing I needed was another lecture. Ben was a good guy, one of my best friends, but he wasn't perfect. And neither was I, so if he started in on me, I doubted I'd hold my tongue.

"What?" I finally blurted; my tone riddled with aggravation. I'd caught the attention of some of the other guys. I wanted to shout that not everything should rest on my shoulders, but when a player got paid as much as I did for my skills, I didn't have much to stand on spouting off otherwise.

"Don't get mad at me because you played like shit."

"Fuck you." I pulled a fresh shirt over my head and slammed my locker.

"What's the matter?" His tone switched from bothersome to concern. "You never play like that."

"I know."

"Are you having a hard time adjusting here?"

"No."

"Is something wrong with your dad?"

I breathed a sigh of relief at his last question. "Thankfully, no."

A heart attack last year almost killed my dad, his years of smoking contributing to the incident. He'd quit right afterward and had been doing well since. But there was always the chance he could succumb to another incident, as he liked to refer to it as. My mother, on the other hand, referred to it as stupidity. She'd been on him to give up the bad habit since my sister and I were kids, but it took staring death in the face to do the trick.

"Do you need to get laid? Are you pent-up?" He laughed at his lame jest, but I wasn't amused. "That's it, isn't it? The great Luke Sorenson needs to get some."

"I got some last night. That's not the issue."

"Play better tomorrow, Sorenson," Andy said as he walked by. I was going to tell him off, but I held my tongue when a glint of a smile crossed over his face right before he disappeared.

"Then what is it?"

Silence was my friend while I pondered whether to inform Ben about my arrangement with Olivia. I teetered between wanting to tell him so I could bounce a few things off him, now and in the future, if need be, and keeping it to myself.

In the end, I divulged everything, even going so far as to say Olivia had been the one woman I'd thought about over the years, the one I compared all others to.

9

OLIVIA

PULLING UP OUTSIDE MY PARENTS' HOUSE, I KILLED THE ENGINE of my white Jeep Wrangler and leaned back in my seat, needing a few extra seconds to prepare myself for what I'd encounter as soon as I walked inside. I hadn't spoken to my mother yet, only having read her texts from last night. She mentioned she had a surprise for me, and I knew what that meant. I had no doubt she'd invited someone over to dinner to join us. Someone for me.

Wearing a jean skirt, a cream-colored sleeveless top, and ballet flats, I looked appropriate for dinner, but there was no way I was going to get all dolled up to meet someone I had no interest in.

As I sat there, working up the strength to deal with my upcoming situation, I couldn't stop thoughts of Luke from infiltrating. Heat bloomed between my legs remembering the way he kissed me, the way he made me feel when we touched. Even when he dropped me off at home afterward, the way he looked at me made me feel like a conquest, and the only woman in the world.

The blend of emotions didn't make a lick of sense. Although, to be fair, the entire night had baffled me, from seeing him again after so long, to agreeing to have sex with him that night, and in the future. We'd agreed not to sleep with other people, but we weren't dating.

A rap on my window startled me out of my daydreaming. Or was it night dreaming, as the sun had started to set? When I looked to see who'd scared me, Mark grinned. Many people had told me there was a family resemblance between us, but the only similarity was the reddish tint to his hair. He was tall like our dad, both standing at six feet even. While they also had a similar thin build, Mark was bulkier.

Grabbing my purse from the seat next to me, I opened my door, pushing him back a step.

"What are you doing here?" I asked.

"Mom invited me. She said she had a date set up for you and thought it would be less awkward for everyone if I was here, too."

"Do you think she'll ever stop fixing me up?"

"Never," he responded, throwing his arm over my shoulder as we walked toward the front porch of the house. "She did this after you broke up with John, and now with Cody." John was the guy I dated right before my most recent ex. He was nice enough, and never cheated like Cody did, but it took me a year after we started dating to figure out we were better off as friends.

Having my older brother here did make me a tad less uncomfortable, but what I would've liked was to have dinner with only my family. Realizing I had to suck it up for the next couple hours, I released one breath after another. And if things *did* get too awkward, I only lived two minutes away.

My parents were lucky enough to find this two-year-old ranch home in the same neighborhood of Henderson we'd lived in since I was born. Once their offer was accepted, I started the process to buy my childhood home.

The front door swung open as I reached for the handle, my mom's beaming smile greeting us.

"Hi, babies." She drew us into a group-type hug before ushering us inside.

"Mom, stop calling us babies. I'm twenty-six and Mark is almost thirty. We're anything but."

"You'll always be my babies. Now stop complaining and help me set the table."

"Where's Dad?" my brother asked, waltzing past us and toward the kitchen, which led to the three-car garage.

"He's tinkering with that car again." My dad had purchased a vintage burgundy 1968 Mustang Fastback six months ago. It was his dream car. And every time I came here to visit, he was messing around with it. "I swear he shows the car more attention than he shows me." She tossed the dishtowel on the counter and opened the oven to peer inside.

"That's not true." My parents were very affectionate toward the other, especially after almost thirty-two years of marriage.

"Well... almost." She winked, her shoulders bouncing in a blasé shrug.

The longest relationship I'd been in was with Cody, which lasted just over a year and a half. And look how that turned out. Would I ever find a love like the one my parents shared? For some unknown reason, Luke's face popped into my head with the thought. Needing to focus on anything other than the man who caused a turmoil of emotions to erupt inside me, I peered over my mom's shoulder and inhaled the aroma of dinner.

"Did you make lasagna?"

"Doug told me it was one of his favorites. And since it's my specialty, I thought it was a perfect choice."

"Doug?"

She turned to look at me, and when she tilted her head, a piece of her chestnut-colored hair fell over her eye. Tucking the strand behind her ear, she smiled, and not the typical mom smile she'd give me when trying to reassure me of something, but the grin that screamed I-know-what's-best-so-don't-start-arguing.

"When are you going to understand I can find my own dates?"

"When was the last time you went out with anyone on your own?" Again, Luke popped into my head, but we hadn't technically gone out, per se. Checking into a hotel and having sex with a guy I hadn't see in ten years wasn't exactly what my mom had been referring to, so I kept my secret all to myself.

"I don't have time. Between work and you setting me up, when do you think I'm going to meet anyone? And thanks, by the way. Martin was a complete bore. He droned on and on about *Star Trek* the entire time. Not to mention, he spits when he talks." Martin was one of my mom's coworker's sons. "It was a complete waste of an evening. I would've enjoyed staring at the wall so much more."

Ella Brighton had this uncanny ability to make people do things they wouldn't normally, her family included. And for as infuriating as she was sometimes, my mom was the best woman I knew.

"Oh, stop exaggerating," she countered, pulling some plates from the cabinet and shoving them at me. "Grab some silverware and set the table, Miss Dramatic." She swatted my butt with the dishtowel.

After the place settings were arranged, I walked toward the garage to see what my dad and brother were up to. But I didn't make it out of the kitchen before the doorbell rang.

"Can you get that?" she asked, removing the tray of lasagna from the oven and placing the pan on top of the stove.

"Do I have to?"

"Olivia Ann." Saying my first and middle name was all it took for me to comply.

"Fine. But I can't guarantee I'll be much company tonight."

"Don't be rude," she shouted after me as I trudged toward the front door. The bell rang once more, the chime irritating me because I had to put on a show for a stranger I'd never see again.

Only the person on the doorstep of my parents' house wasn't a stranger at all.

10

LUKE

"What are you doing here?" Olivia's eyes were so big she reminded me of a cartoon character. A sexy, begging-to-be-kissed cartoon character.

"Surprise." I moved to take a step inside, but she blocked me from entering. "You're not going to let me in?"

"Not until you tell me what you're doing here. How do you even know where my parents live?"

Her stunned expression had waned since she answered the door, but she was still a bit dumbstruck. I didn't blame her, though. I did just show up out of the blue.

"Luke. Glad you could make it." Mark walked up behind Olivia, but she was still blocking the doorway. He tapped her arm. "Don't be rude. Let him in."

"Yeah, Ollie. Let me in."

"Ollie," he repeated. "No one has called her that in years."

"That's because it was my special nickname for her," I said, my eyes veering to my friend before landing back on the gorgeous woman in front of me. With some light prodding from her older brother, she finally took a step back so I could enter. After shaking hands with Mark, whom I'd run into earlier today at a liquor store of all places, I leaned in and kissed Olivia's cheek right before I wrapped her in a huge hug. Pressing my lips to her ear, I whispered, "I miss being inside you." She gasped the same time I released her. "How long has it been?" The only words Mark heard me speak were the last five.

"What?"

"I asked how long it's been since we've seen each other."

"Oh." Her attention bounced between me and her brother. "Um... I... I don't know." She barely managed to get her words out, her flustered state not going unnoticed by Mark.

"What's wrong with you? Why are you acting so weird?" he asked. "Is it because that guy will be here soon? Don't be nervous. Luke and I got you. We'll take some of the pressure off." He wrapped his arm around her shoulders and kissed her temple. They'd always had such a close relationship, and it was nice to see that aspect of their lives hadn't changed.

"Who's coming over?" I asked, pretending not to know she was being set up on a blind date.

"My mom invited some guy over to dinner tonight to meet Olivia."

"Doug," she uttered. Her attention was on her sibling when she spoke. "Mom said his name is Doug."

"Doug," I repeated. I didn't like the sound of his name.

"Yes, Doug. And don't either of you say anything embarrassing."

With her shock at my intrusion finally gone, she followed Mark farther into the house. And I had the pleasure of walking behind her. When I deemed my buddy was out of earshot, I grabbed her waist and stopped her in her tracks, resting my lips near her ear like I'd done a few minutes ago.

"Do you like that I shaved?"

"It doesn't make a difference to me." She kept her back to me, but I could tell her breathing had quickened.

"It will when my I bury my head between your legs again."

She threw me a glare over her shoulder, but there was intrigue laced behind her eyes, even though she tried to hide it.

"You're impossible." She swatted at my hand.

"Impossibly horny."

Thankfully, my response was only meant for Olivia's ears because her mom had just turned the corner and was headed right for me. The woman looked the same as she did the last time I saw her. There was no doubt where her daughter got her looks from.

"Hi, Mrs. B." I opened my arms and she walked right into them.

"Oh my God, Luke. This is such a wonderful surprise." She pulled back and looked me over from head to toe. "You're all grown up now." *Is that a tear in her eye?* "I can't believe it. You're so handsome. But you always were." Her palm cupped my freshly shaved cheek. "Isn't he handsome, Olivia?"

"He's all right," she rebutted, glaring at me from behind her mom.

"Oh, stop it." Mrs. B never took her eyes from mine. "She's teasing."

"I know."

"I'm not," Olivia said as she walked away from us.

"You know, Jack and I are so proud of you. I don't follow sports, but I've watched a few of your games." She ruffled my hair as she led me toward the kitchen. "You're so good."

"Thanks. I'm thankful I get to play." I didn't know what else to say other than the truth. It'd been a dream of mine to play professional soccer, and since the day that goal came to fruition, I never took my opportunity for granted, no matter how famous I got or how much money I made.

"Wait until Jack finds out you're here. He's going to be so excited. And please humor him when he bombards you with questions."

"I will."

And bombard me he did, but I enjoyed every praise and every question he threw my way. He'd been like a second father to me growing up, and to hear the pride in his voice when he told me how happy he was for me... well, let's just say I got a bit emotional. But luckily, I hid it well.

I was in the garage admiring his vintage Mustang when the doorbell rang. Olivia had been in here with us but left when her mom called her into the kitchen. No doubt she sent her to welcome her date. Mrs. B popped her head back in and told the three of us that dinner would be ready in five minutes and for us to wash up beforehand.

"Where's the bathroom?"

"I'll show you," Mark said, jerking his chin toward the door. I followed him, the entire time trying to digest how I felt about sitting at the same table as someone who had been brought here purposely to meet the woman I'd had sex with last night. Sure, our circumstance was unusual, to put it lightly, but no way did I want her engaging with some other guy, even if all it turned out to be was polite banter. Was it too much to ask that all her attention be on me the entire time I was here? Was I being irrational? If I voiced either question to anyone other than myself, the answer would undoubtedly be a resounding yes.

After finishing up in the bathroom, I opened the door and took a single step into the hallway but stopped when Olivia came into view. She had her back to me, mumbling something under her breath, but she stood too far away for me to make out anything she said. Her body language, however, screamed she was weary of something. Or possibly someone. Was she upset I'd showed up tonight? Or had she gotten a look at the guy her mom invited to dinner and was repulsed? I hoped it was the latter.

After shifting from one foot to the other repeatedly, she finally turned around, only to catch me staring at her. Her hand flew to rest on her chest after a quick inhale, and right as her mouth opened to either berate me for scaring her or say something else entirely, I rushed toward her and grasped her wrist, pulling her into the bathroom with me.

I slammed the door shut behind her, locking it so she couldn't escape. While I figured out what to say, I snatched the opportunity to ogle her a bit more. The sleeveless top she had on dipped in the front, but not so much to show cleavage of any sort. But I knew what was underneath that shirt. The image of her hardened nipples popped into my head, and I remembered how she squirmed when I lavished them with my tongue.

We stood close, her head resting against the door I pinned her to. She had to crane her neck to look into my eyes. Only a few seconds had passed since I dragged her in here, but it felt like an hour.

"What are you doing?" she finally asked.

"Are you mad at me?" I had no idea the question was going to come flying out of my mouth until it did.

She nibbled on the inside of her cheek, stalling for time before answering. As long as she didn't immediately say yes, I could live with whatever her response ended up being.

"You never answered my question."

Now I was confused. "What question?"

"Why are you here? How did you know where my parents lived? And can you move back? You're making me claustrophobic."

"First off, that's three questions. And you're not claustrophobic."

"Just move back." She shoved at me, and I retreated two steps, giving her the space she wanted.

"I ran into Mark today, and he invited me over."

"What you're telling me is that you happened to run into my brother on the same day you knew I had a potential blind date? Which is also the day after we agreed to keep hooking up? Don't you think that's a little coincidental?"

"It's not coincidental. It's fate." She rolled her eyes, but the faintest twitch of her cheek told me she wasn't all that upset with me.

"Why didn't you give me a heads-up you'd be here? You could've texted me."

"I wanted to surprise you."

"You wanted to ambush me."

I made a noncommittal noise with my throat because I couldn't disagree.

"That's what I thought," she said, attempting to spin toward the door to leave. "We have to get out there or they're going to come looking for us, and I don't think it's a good idea if anyone catches us locked in a bathroom together. As far as my family is concerned, tonight is the first time we've seen each other since you left." When Olivia said the word *left*, her shoulders slumped. Could she be upset with me for going away to college? I'd meant to keep in touch, but I'd been busy with school and getting drafted. As the years passed, I thought it would be awkward to reach out after so much time had gone by, even though I thought about her a lot.

But when I saw her last night, it was like no time had passed at all.

I turned her back to face me before she could leave. "Kiss me."

"No." Her response was immediate, but the way she looked at my mouth told me she wanted to say yes. So, I pressed.

"Come on. You know you want to." Pulling her into me caused her to stumble. "I need a taste before you make me go out there and endure watching some other guy fawn all over you. What does he look like, by the way? Do you think he's attractive?"

"He's cute."

Her tone was blasé, and I couldn't decipher if she told the truth.

With her hands resting on my chest, I wondered if she could feel my heartbeat thrum wildly beneath her fingertips. If I placed my hand on her chest, would I cause the same reaction for her?

"Is he more attractive than me?" Why was I torturing myself?

"I'm not stroking your ego, Luke." My inability to read her drove me insane. Was she messing with me? Goading me? Purposely making me jealous?

"You better not be stroking anything on him either. Remember we agreed not to have sex with anyone else while we're doing this." I waved my finger between us.

"Oh my God. I just met him. I wouldn't sleep with him anyway, even if we weren't doing this." She motioned back and forth like I'd done, but with a bit more exaggeration. "I don't make it a habit of sleeping with strangers."

"If I wasn't at the bar last night, you would've. You told Brooke as much." The simple thought that she could've taken some other guy, a stranger, to a hotel room didn't sit well with me. But my dislike of the fictional situation was nothing compared to Olivia's reaction when I brought it up.

She pointed her finger in my face, her expression morphing from slight annoyance to robust irritation. "That's none of your business." She spoke slowly to get her point across, and it was received loud and clear. "Besides, I don't know if I would've followed through with it."

"You can't now."

The pull of her brows and the narrowing of her eyes amused me because it meant I'd gotten to her, as I typically managed to do.

"I'm aware."

Her voice raised slightly with her comment. In the wake of her realizing she shouldn't have spoken so loudly, we stared at each other, waiting for someone to knock on the door. When no one did, I thought it was a good time to ask for that kiss again, but in a more subtle way.

"I like your skirt."

A permanent frown line was going to mar her gorgeous face if she kept looking at me like that.

"Thanks."

"And your shirt."

"Thank yo—"

"I'd prefer both on the floor, but I can wait."

"You're an ass."

One good shove and she managed to knock me back a step, enough for her to turn and unlock the door. Before she escaped, however, I shifted her hair to the side and pressed my lips to her neck.

Ignoring her comment, I threw one of my own at her, hoping to disarm her before we joined everyone else for dinner.

"I can't wait for round two."

"Keep it up and there won't be a round two."

"A deal is a deal, woman. You can't back out." I wanted to stay locked in this room all night bantering, but she had other plans, which included escaping.

She shoved me back, this time by using one of her greatest assets. Her ass.

The click of the lock signified we were done with our back and forth, but I needed a few extra seconds. I gripped her hips and pressed my arousal against her. I swore I got hard when she met me at the front door.

"Kiss me and I'll be on my best behavior." Thinking of whatever I could to get what I wanted seemed to be the direction I went in.

"Who are you kidding?"

"I will."

Olivia peered at me over her shoulder, the corner of her mouth curving up slightly. "You do realize I didn't just meet you, right?· I know you, more than I want to." *What does that mean?* I didn't dare ask for fear her answer would break whatever spell I was under.

Mark's voice echoed from a couple of rooms away, asking where Olivia and I were, putting a slight damper on my mood. The guy cockblocked me and didn't even know it. Okay, maybe that was an exaggeration, but he'd thrown me into an irritated mood. If this woman would let me kiss her, I could function halfway decent throughout dinner. But I had a feeling she was going to remain obstinate.

"One kiss?"

"Luke." Her saying my name like a warning pushed me to finally stop asking.

"Fine. But I'm getting my fill tomorrow." I slapped her on the ass for good measure, and when she didn't berate me for the action, I smiled. "Now let's go have some fun."

11

OLIVIA

LUKE FELL INTO STEP BESIDE ME AS WE WALKED DOWN THE SHORT hallway and entered the kitchen. His hand brushed against mine several times, and all I wanted to do was shove it under my skirt and demand he thrill me, but I did no such thing. The guy was starting to get under my skin, and it wasn't necessarily all bad, which wasn't what I expected.

"There you are." My mom rounded the island and shoved a wooden salad bowl filled with the fixings at me. "Can you put this on the table, honey?" Before I walked away, her gaze landed on Luke before veering back to me. The slight flicker of her eyes didn't give much away, but some thought about the two of us might've formed in her head. "And don't be rude, Olivia. Go talk to Doug."

Luke made a noise behind me, but I refused to look at him. I was too busy trying to bring my body's reaction to him back under control. If I failed, I had no idea how the rest of the evening was going to pan out.

"You don't want to keep your date waiting," he whispered in my ear as he passed, his tone a mix of playfulness and jealousy.

When I entered the dining room, Doug was standing near

Mark, chatting about whatever it was guys talked about. When he saw me, the corners of his mouth kicked up. He really was cute. I hadn't lied about that to Luke. His dark blond hair was cropped close to his head in a style that worked on him. And his smile matched the warmth of his dark brown eyes.

I returned the grin as I placed the salad bowl in the center of the table. But when he looked past me with widened eyes, I turned to see what had caught his attention. Although, I should've known. Luke was famous, but to me he was the guy who grew up two doors down. He was also the guy I'd loved, but that was my little secret.

"Luke Sorenson?" Doug's voice rose a notch, his legs propelling him toward Luke as he spoke. "I'm a huge fan."

"Thanks." The two men shook hands, and for a moment my date forgot all about me, which I should've been thankful for as I wasn't interested in him in a romantic sense.

"What are you doing here?"

"I'm an old family friend. Decided to drop by for dinner and catch up."

I walked by them but didn't get far when Luke snatched my hand and pulled me into him, wrapping his arm around my waist a second later. Anything at all could come flying out of his mouth, and if it was something inappropriate or embarrassing, I'd have to contain my reaction enough so as not to draw any suspicion from anyone as to what might be going on between the two of us. Or were all these thoughts simply my own paranoia over what I knew to be a strictly sexual relationship with us? I closed my eyes briefly, chastising myself for overthinking yet another scenario that involved the guy holding me close.

Instead of Luke uttering something that might've made me angry or uncomfortable, all he did was kiss my temple. The action was innocent enough to an onlooker such as Doug, but I read it for what it was, which was Luke laying claim to me in front of another male.

I wiggled myself away from him, flashing my date a quick smile before heading back to the kitchen. As I rounded the corner, I barreled into my dad. He grabbed my shoulders in surprise, smiling big right before he pulled me into a hug. I'd just spent some time with him in the garage, along with Mark and Luke, but there was something about his embrace that comforted me. Soothed some of my twisting nerves that wouldn't settle.

When he pulled back, he looked at me with a hint of compassion. "I tried to talk your mom out of setting you up again, but she wouldn't listen. You know her, though. When she's intent on something, nothing will get in her way." He tapped the end of my nose playfully.

"I know. It's why I didn't give her too much of an argument this time. I figured I'd humor her. Like you said, no point in fighting it."

"I'm surprised she hasn't tried to hook you up with Luke yet." He laughed, thinking his comment was completely off base. If he only knew how many positions the man put me into last night, he wouldn't be so amused.

"I doubt she'd take it there." If my mom caught even the slightest whiff there was something between me and Luke, she'd jump all over it. I had to be careful tonight not to ignite any part of her imagination when it came to him.

"What's this Doug guy like? Your mom can't stop raving about him."

"I haven't really gotten a chance to talk to him yet. He's a fan of Luke's, that much I know."

"Who isn't?" My dad kissed the top of my head. "I better change my shirt before your mom gets all riled up."

As if she knew we were talking about her, she walked up behind us, pulling open one of the drawers and grabbing a spatula.

"Dinner is on the table. Let's go, you two." She turned to

walk away but not before focusing on her husband's grease-stained shirt. "Jack, hurry up and change." With a huff, she was gone.

"And fix your hair, too," I teased.

"What's wrong with my hair?" He ran his fingers through his salt-and-pepper strands, making it worse. I swatted his hand away and tamped down the wayward section that had been sticking up. "All good?"

"Gorgeous. Now go change before she has a conniption."

There were six places set at the table, two on each side and one at each end. My parents took the end seats, as was typical, and I took one of the empty seats next to my mom, figuring Doug would sit next to me. But someone beat him to it. My date was so enthralled with Luke being at the same table, he didn't seem to mind he wasn't going to be sitting next to the woman he'd been set up with tonight.

Once Luke was situated, I leaned in, being sure to keep my voice low when I asked, "What do you think you're doing?"

He answered me right away, but with a voice loud enough for everyone to hear. "What do you mean?"

"What's going on?" Mark asked, leaning forward and scooping out a piece of lasagna for himself.

I replied, "Nothing," the same time Luke answered, "Ollie asked what I thought I was doing." Mortification spiraled through me, and I'd never wanted to smack him more.

"About what?" This time the question came from my dad.

"I'm not sure," Luke answered, scratching the side of his clean-shaven face. I had to admit that while I thought the beard was sexy, seeing his entire face only made him that much more handsome. Did he really shave because he wanted to see if having smooth skin when he went down on me again would help further along my goal?

"Honey?"

"What?" I wasn't quite sure which one of my parents called

for my attention, lost to the image of Luke's head wedged between my thighs.

"Are you all right?" My mother's sole attention was on me, her frown indicative of her concern.

"Sorry. I don't know what's gotten into me."

"I know who's going to get into you soon," Luke whispered, placing his hand on my thigh beneath the table. The contact made me fidget in my seat, but I didn't believe anyone noticed. Or at least I hoped they didn't.

Gripping his fingers tightly, I tried to dislodge his hold on me, but he refused to let go. After the third attempt, I gave up, assuming if I continued, I'd only end up making things worse and causing a scene.

Leaning over him to get a piece of garlic bread, I whispered, "If you do anything to me, I'll kill you." My words passed through gritted teeth. The sickly-sweet smile on his face suggested he could go either way with my threat. I wouldn't put it past him to rile me further by teasing me. His hand had already inched up my leg.

"Can you come into the shop early tomorrow? We had a drop off tonight right at closing, and I could really use your help." My dad was the one talking, but because my head was down, I didn't know if he was speaking to me or my brother. "Olivia, did you hear me?" *Looks like it's me.*

"What time?" I asked, ripping off a piece of bread and shoving it in my mouth as gracefully as I could manage.

"Seven thirty."

"Okay." An hour earlier than I planned on being there wasn't the end of the world.

From the corner of my eye, I noticed Luke had turned to look at me. He inhaled, and I waited for him to say something, but my mom beat him to it.

"Doug, did I tell you Olivia is a mechanic? She works with my husband and my son at the family-owned garage."

"Really? That's interesting. Are there a lot of women in that field?" I assumed he directed his question at me, so I raised my eyes to his, attempting to ignore the surge of heat Luke's hand caused.

"More than you would think." Truth be told, I didn't know the stats on female mechanics, but I knew of another garage across town that employed one.

"I didn't know you worked with your dad and Mark," Luke said, squeezing my leg when I didn't respond right away.

"You didn't ask."

A forkful of cheesy goodness filled my mouth before I accidentally dove into the territory of the lack of subjects we discussed last night. All our focus had been on sex and nothing else. And it would remain that way. We weren't dating. We had one goal to accomplish. Mixing in everyday life would only muddy the waters.

He mumbled something next to me, but he also shoved food in his face, so I couldn't be sure what he'd said. Knowing him, it was probably something snarky.

Needing to be somewhat engaged with the guy my mom dragged here tonight, I asked him a question about himself.

"My mom tells me you're a nursing student. How are you liking it?"

"It's radiology."

"Oh, sorry."

"No big deal. And I'm happy with the job so far. Ella has been really kind, showing me around the hospital and introducing me to everyone." Doug leaned back, his eyes bouncing from my mom to me and back again. When she patted the top of his hand, he twitched in his seat, his gaze lingering on her longer than appropriate.

Was he interested in her?

"Everyone there loves him. He's such a nice guy." She smiled at him, and the look he gave her in return solidified my assumption. It was like she was the sun and he needed her to survive. Okay, maybe not something as dramatic, but Doug had the hots for Ella Brighton. A beautiful, much older, and married mother of two grown children. And God love her, she was clueless.

"So, Doug, what makes a young, single guy accept a dinner invitation to be set up on a blind date? Can't get a woman on your own?"

"Luke." My tone was a mix of shock and reprimand.

"What?" He shrugged and gestured toward our guest. "He knows I'm playing." He wasn't playing, not at all. He was being rude.

"That's okay." Doug peeked at my mom before answering. "I work a lot, so I don't get to go out much and meet people. But when Ella couldn't stop talking about Olivia, I was intrigued. And when she showed me a picture...." His voice drifted off at the end.

"I told you she was beautiful."

"She is." His attention moved from my mom to me. "You are."

My cheeks heated at the compliment, or was the reaction due to Luke's hand pushing my skirt farther up my leg. His fingers fell between my thighs, close to the edge of my underwear. Again, I tried to remove his hand, but he wouldn't budge. I kept my irritation at his brazenness on a simmer, because otherwise I'd end up drawing everyone's attention. At one point, I tried to turn sideways in my seat, but he only dug his fingers into my leg, holding me in place, his forefinger managing to glide over the top of the silk material which covered the most intimate part of me.

"You're sweet. Thank you."

Again, Luke mumbled next to me, but no one else noticed.

Over the next twenty minutes, the conversation ranged from talk about Luke's skills on the field, to our work at the shop, to gossip about Mom and Doug's coworkers, mainly drama with a couple of the nurses and one of the doctors. Apparently, he was sleeping with them, and they didn't know about each other.

I kept a close watch on our dinner guest, and sure enough, every now and again he looked at my mom with adoration. He definitely had a thing for her, which was probably why he never asked to switch seats with Luke when we first sat down to dinner. He didn't want to lose his seat next to her.

After everyone praised the dinner, she rose from her seat to get the dessert, chocolate mint brownies with a scoop of vanilla ice cream. But Luke pulled me to my feet before I had a chance to object.

"Let us get it. You've already done so much already." He dragged me into the kitchen, and I was sure the look of surprise on my face was comical, had anyone been paying attention. But everyone was chatting among themselves.

Yanking my hand from his once we were out of sight, I threw a glare in his direction.

"Could you be more obvious?"

Luke pulled six plates from the cupboard once I'd pointed to where they were kept. "I thought we could help out."

"Yeah, right." My hip rested against the edge of the island, my arms crossed over my chest.

"I don't like the way that guy is looking at you," he said, his comment coming completely out of left field. If he only knew Doug didn't have an ounce of interest in me, he'd be able to rein in his jealousy. But because I wanted to torment him like he'd been doing to me since he showed up tonight, I didn't say a word about the guy's infatuation with my mom.

"We are kind of on a date, so it's a good thing he's interested." A smug smile spread over my face, widening when Luke dropped the ice cream scooper on the counter and stared at me with his mouth open.

But he didn't say anything, instead cutting into the tray of brownies with force, slapping them on a plate and sliding them toward me. The flex of his biceps and the tick in his jaw screamed he wanted to respond, but he kept his mouth shut. Perhaps he realized that if he caused an unnecessary commotion, I'd cancel our little arrangement. Or maybe he was at a loss for words. If I had to bet, I'd guess it was the former.

12

LUKE

"What are you looking at?" Mark asked, coming up behind me and startling me. He moved me to the side so he could see what had caught my attention, making a noise with his throat when he saw Olivia and Doug standing by his car. "What do you think of him?"

"I don't like him."

He slapped me on the back. "He didn't seem so bad."

"I don't like him," I repeated.

"Staring at them like an overbearing father isn't going to make him leave any quicker. Come back in and have a beer. Relax."

If he only knew what I did to his sister last night, *overbearing father* wouldn't have been the phrase he would've used.

Tearing myself away from the window, I followed him to the kitchen to grab a cold one, then to the living room where his parents sat together on the large leather sofa.

It was nice to see them as much in love as when we were kids. I hoped to find that someday. I wasn't anywhere near ready to settle down for the long haul, but in the future, I hoped I would be. Olivia's image popped into my head at the thought, but I discarded it because the notion was crazy. She barely tolerated me as it was. There was no way she'd want to be with me. Lost to the various thoughts floating around inside my head, I never heard her approach. When she plopped down next to her parents, she tucked her legs underneath her, briefly casting a curious glance my way.

Her mom leaned forward. "What did you think of Doug?"

The smile that appeared on Olivia's face pissed me off, and I struggled to keep my reaction hidden.

"He seems nice enough. I didn't really get a chance to talk to him much, though. Then again, it doesn't matter because he's not interested in me."

"Did he tell you that?"

"No. I was the one who told him I wasn't interested in dating since I recently got out of a relationship."

Her mom huffed and leaned back, but I straightened in my seat, thankful I didn't have to worry about some guy sniffing around my woman.

My woman? Where did that come from?

"What makes you think he's not interested in you?" Mr. B asked, glancing at his daughter briefly before returning his attention to the shark documentary they'd been watching.

"Because he likes Mom," she blurted.

"What?" Mrs. B's voice rose an octave in surprise. "No, he doesn't." Her face reddened slightly. Did she assume the same thing, but played it off as nothing? Or was she as shocked to hear the news like everyone else?

"Oh, he does, Mom. He kept looking at you like a lost puppy." She pointed at her. "He's got a huge crush on you."

I'd been paying so much attention to the back and forth between the two women that I missed when Mr. B squared his shoulders, turning to stare at his wife.

"Is she telling the truth, Ella? Does that kid like you?" His voice dipped low when he asked the question.

"Of course not. Olivia's playing around." Her brows drew inward, and her mouth was slightly parted, her expression displaying either her confusion or her acknowledgement. I couldn't readily decipher.

"I'm not. He likes you. You better watch how much attention you give him at work. You don't want a stalker." Olivia laughed, but there was nothing funny about the way Mr. B continued to tense up. And Mark mirrored his reaction. Serious expression, posture rigid.

"Am I going to have to start coming to your job?" her husband asked, his question bordering on anger. "Do I have to have a talk with him?"

"No," she hurriedly responded, looking at everyone, including me, before turning back to the man sitting next to her. "Even if he *is* interested, I'm not, of course. If Olivia is right, it's nothing more than a crush. He's new and I've been nice to him. That's all."

Mr. B chewed on his bottom lip, his gaze never leaving his wife. I could only imagine what ran through his mind. If that was me and I found out some young guy was hot for my wife of over thirty years, well... I didn't know what I'd do honestly. But I wouldn't be happy about it, and there would be no way I'd let things go without confronting said guy.

Instead of saying anything more, he stood and walked out of the living room. All of us could see he was upset.

"Thanks, Olivia," her mom said right before she followed him.

"You better be right about Doug and not just stirring things up to get the focus off you." Mark's tone was bordering harsh.

"I'm not. And I'm right about this."

Several minutes of silence dredged by. If her parents were arguing, they weren't doing so loudly.

"I'm going to call it a night." Olivia stood and stretched her arms above her head, the bottom of her shirt rising an inch. "Gotta be at work early tomorrow."

"I'll walk you out," I offered, shaking Mark's hand when he also stood, thumping on his back after pulling him in for a half hug. We'd stayed in touch over the years, but not as much as I would have liked. Life happened and took us in different directions. And while I'd occasionally asked about his sister, her occupation never came up. Which was why I was shocked to hear she worked at the garage.

"I'm fine. You stay. Catch up."

"I insist."

"No, really. I don't need you to walk me to my car."

"I'm going to anyway."

"Jesus, Liv, let him walk you out," Mark said, shaking his head and sighing. "And we'll make plans to hang out soon, Luke." He smacked my shoulder twice before exiting the room, leaving me alone with his sister.

Her hushed tone when she spoke again excited me, reminding me we shared a secret. A sexy secret.

"Stop trying to invade my life."

"I'm not. I just want to make sure you get to your car okay."

"Liar." Her steps were hurried as she advanced toward the door.

"You're not going to say goodbye to your parents?" I was three paces behind her, briefly forgetting how fast she walked when she was annoyed.

"They have their own thing going on because of my big mouth. I'll call my mom tomorrow and I'll see my dad at work."

I reached for her arm to slow her down, but she yanked it away the second I made contact. "Ollie, slow down." I expected her to yell at me for using the nickname she hated, but she didn't say a word, the gravel beneath her shoes crunching as she walked to her Jeep. Or should I say, power-walked to her Jeep?

Only when the driver door was opened, and she had one leg inside, did she turn toward me.

"Go home, Luke."

There was something indescribable about the look on her face. She was either annoyed with me, or she was slightly amused. The purse of her lips didn't solidly land on either option.

"Can I come over?" I asked, hoping her expression landed more on the slightly amused side. "I thought we could... you know." My eyes slowly skated over the length of her.

"No, I don't. What do you mean?" *Was she serious?* Gone was any look of possible amusement, her expression deadpanning immediately before she asked her question.

"You know," I repeated, tilting my head to the side in slight confusion. Her eyebrows rose. "Sex."

"And why would we have sex?"

"So I can try again to make you come." Saying the words made my dick twitch. Olivia must've known because her focus swung toward my crotch briefly before her eyes lifted back to mine.

"Whatever image you have in your head, keep it there for next time." She pushed me back so she could close her door, and I let her because I was so wrapped up in the mental vision I had of her naked, with her legs spread, begging for me to fuck her.

Olivia drove off and I was left standing in her parents' driveway with a raging hard-on.

13

OLIVIA

"I want someone else to look at it. Someone with experience."

The asshat standing ten feet away peered at me as if I was beneath him, his greasy palms clutching the edge of the counter. Sweat dripped down the sides of his pudgy face, the condescending look he threw at me making me want to punch him right in his fat nose. But I kept my temper in check, albeit barely.

"I assure you, sir, I have more than enough experience to look at your vehicle." He pulled up in a red 1962 Jaguar XKE Roadster. It was gorgeous, yet I doubted he appreciated the beauty of the car. To him it was probably a purchase to help him through his midlife crisis. To be honest, I had no idea how he even fit behind the wheel.

"Do you even know how to check the oil on a car like that?"

"Do you?" I countered, failing to keep the contempt from my voice like I'd planned.

"I want to speak to your boss."

The shade that stole over his face matched that of his car, and since causing customers to have heart attacks wasn't good business sense, I walked into the garage and tapped my brother on the shoulder, even though he wasn't technically the boss. But our dad had been called out on a tow. Mark was busy replacing a manifold gasket on a ten-year-old Toyota and looked a bit annoyed when I interrupted him. He was a perfectionist when it came to work, and if he was in the middle of a job, he didn't like being disturbed. But I didn't have another choice.

"What's up?" He brushed a strand of hair out of his face, getting a smudge of oil near his brow.

"Some jagoff doesn't want me looking at his car," I huffed. "Can you please go deal with him?"

"These fucking guys." He squeezed my shoulder in a sign of solidarity. "Don't pay any attention to that shit, Liv. You're a great mechanic. You might even be better than me."

"Might be?"

"Don't be smug." He chuckled, heading toward the front office. If the potential customer made a derogatory comment about me to him, I had no doubt he'd tell the guy where he could shove his car. It wasn't like we needed the business. We were jam-packed with appointments every day.

Ten minutes later, my brother walked back into the garage, holding a set of keys. The Jaguar's keys. I wiggled my fingers for him to give them to me.

"He said third gear keeps sticking, and he thinks it's leaking oil." He tossed me the keys. "He's still here, waiting for a ride. Wait until he leaves to pull it in. And Brooke is here."

As if on cue, my best friend waltzed into the garage, shifting her long dark hair to one side. It was nearing one in the afternoon, and she was dressed in a cream-and-blue-striped sundress, which would be fine except I thought she had work this afternoon.

"No matter how many times I see you in those things," she said, twirling her finger in the air, "I can't get used to the sight."

"You don't like my overalls?"

"Not particularly."

"They're not fashionable enough for you?" I did a slow spin with my arms out.

"Not in the least."

"They're not supposed to be trendy. I wear them to protect my clothes. Plus, they're handy." I reached into my pockets and pulled out a screwdriver, a pair of pliers, and a wrench.

"And *I'm* the lesbian," she said with a laugh. Brooke glanced around the garage to gauge the proximity of my brother before opening her mouth again. "I'm dying to know what happened the other night. You texted he didn't... you didn't... you know." She wiggled her well-manicured brows and pursed her lips. Her coded talk was an extra precaution so Mark wouldn't catch wind of our conversation.

"Goal not accomplished," I responded. "But I did have a lot of fun trying."

"Oh well. At least now you know for sure."

Brooke and I had only texted since I hooked up with Luke, and I told her I'd fill her in on everything as soon as I could. This was the first chance either of us had to really talk. And there was so much more I had to tell her, starting with the deal I made with him.

Various ways to phrase what I wanted to say next flitted through my mind, but the one I ended up voicing was the bluntest of them all.

"He's agreed to continue and try to make me orgasm, and in exchange I've agreed to be his date to Heather's wedding in a couple months."

Brooke had been checking out some of the tools on a nearby rolling cart when she dropped a socket wrench, the clanging sound seemingly amplifying what I'd told her.

"Wait a second. You two agreed to do what?"

I leaned in closer, lowering my voice to barely above a whisper. "He offered to continue to help me out," I said, widening my eyes and tilting my head, "if I agreed to be his date to his sister's wedding."

Her gaze bounced from the ceiling, to where Mark was working on the Toyota, and finally back to me, her ear-splitting smile matching the blend of excitement and nervousness traveling through me. I was opening myself up to Luke, literally and figuratively, and depending on my mood or the time of day, I wasn't sure which feeling to land on.

"I'm pissed at you."

"Okayyyy." I drew out the two-syllable word in my confusion. "Why?"

"This type of information should've been shared immediately. Not two days later." She smacked my arm.

"It's not something I want to put in a text. And this is the first time I've seen you. And speaking of, aren't you supposed to be at work?"

"Not until tonight. I switched shifts with Angie. She and her fiancé are going away for a few days, and they didn't want to wait until tomorrow to leave."

Brooke was a blackjack dealer at Caesars Palace, which is why I questioned her attire because she had a uniform requirement for her job, one she didn't love. But the amount of money she made during any given shift outweighed the lack of fashion her attire projected.

"Is he really above average?" she blurted, but I shouldn't have been surprised. I was waiting for her to probe me for more information. My only response was to nod vigorously. "And does he know how to use it?"

"Absolutely. And his tongue. And his hands." If I wasn't careful, I was going to act all swoony and embarrass myself. Remembering that Luke was a pain in the ass, and I didn't like him all that much, and our arrangement was purely sexual, I flattened my rising enthusiasm.

"So he's not just a gorgeous face and a famous, wealthy

athlete." Her statement required no rebuttal or affirmation. She simply stated facts.

I pulled her closer to the office so my brother wouldn't accidentally overhear us. For the next ten minutes, I filled her in on all the ways Luke tried to "help me out," as well as what happened last night when he showed up at my parents' house, including how my date had a thing for my mom.

I was in the middle of telling her how Luke was trying to convince me to let him come over last night when my phone vibrated in my pocket.

"Is that him?"

I pulled my cell out and turned it over to look at the screen. Sure enough, it was him calling. Didn't he ever hear of texting first?

Hitting the green phone icon, I said, "Hold on a sec," before turning the phone inward to say goodbye to Brooke, but she just stood there. When I frowned, she told me to put the call on speaker. She wanted to congratulate him for a good effort the other night. I swatted at her hand when she tried to grab the device from me.

"Do you want me to call you back?" he asked.

"No. I'm saying goodbye to Brooke." My best friend moved closer.

"Did you tell her what a great job I did the other night?"

"Not good enough," Brooke answered, standing so close now she heard him talking on the other end of the line.

"I'm going to redeem myself," he rebutted, and I sighed. I should give the phone to her so they could have their own conversation.

I kissed her cheek before gently shoving her to leave.

"You're no fun." She pouted, waving to Mark before she finally walked toward the exit.

"Are you still there?" he asked, the noise in the background fading in and out.

"I'm here." Silence drifted over the line, and I wasn't sure what else to say. If I counted to five, and he still hadn't spoken, I would. I only made it to three.

"I'm calling to see if we can get together tonight."

Initially, I was going to stall for time, but what was the point? We had a deal, and if we barely did the deed, how was I ever going to hope to achieve my ultimate goal?

"I'm free. What time?"

"I was thinking I could come over to your place around six. Will you be done with work by then?"

"I get off at five, so that time will work."

"Here's to hoping you get off twice today."

"That is the plan, right?" To have this kind of conversation with the guy I used to obsess about years ago was a little surreal. "But I think we should go back to a hotel."

"I disagree. Hotels are impersonal and this has to be as personal as possible. It's sex. You and me. Fucking. With the goal of trying to make you come before or while I'm deep inside you." The way his voice dipped toward the end made me swallow my breath. "We're doing this at your place or mine. I vote for your house because you should be comfortable."

I took everything he said into consideration, and in the end, I agreed with his point. I would feel more comfortable in my space, not that I would be opposed to his house at some point either.

"Okay. Come by my house at six to have sex."

"Did you just make a joke?"

"I'm in a good mood."

"Is it because of me?" His question was filled with hope.

"Not particularly." I only half lied. "I get to work on a 1962 Jaguar XKE Roadster. The customer doesn't know I'll be handling the repairs, but Mark and I will keep that little secret."

"Why?"

"Because he's one of those guys who doesn't trust me because I'm a woman."

"Did he say that to you?" There was an edge to his voice I wasn't used to hearing. It was something akin to anger.

"That was the gist of it. I had Mark deal with him. No use in losing business because the guy is a prick. Besides, I really wanted to work on his car."

"I still can't believe you're a mechanic. That's wild. And sexy as hell."

"If you saw my overalls, you wouldn't think so."

"But I know what's underneath them."

When I didn't respond to his comment, he cleared his throat. Not long after, we both spoke at the same time.

"You go," I urged.

"I was only going to say that I have to get back to practice. I'll see you at six."

After we hung up, I focused all my attention on the red Jaguar, hoping it was the distraction I needed to calm the swirl of nerves in my belly.

14

LUKE

"I THOUGHT YOU STOOD ME UP." I WALKED TOWARD OLIVIA'S JEEP, standing next to her door before she even shut the engine off.

"How would I manage to do that?" she asked, flinging open her door and almost knocking into me. "It's not like I wouldn't come home." She hopped out before turning to reach back in, leaning over and grabbing something off the passenger seat. "A part I was waiting on didn't come until four. Sorry."

The dark gray overalls she wore didn't detract from her scrumptious backside. My hand was already midway through the air before I could stop myself, connecting with her ass cheek seconds later.

"Ow!" she yelled, backing up, and right into my crotch. "What the hell, Luke?"

"It's those overalls. They got me all hot and bothered." She glanced down at herself.

"Stop playing."

"I've only just begun." I followed her to her porch, tapping my foot when she dropped her keys. "I'm horny, woman."

"It's not about you, *man*."

"Touché."

Upon entering her house, I noticed a few things were different from the last time I'd been in here. Granted, ten years had passed, and it had been her family home. But now it was all hers, and she'd put her stamp on it. The wall color had gone from a medium-grade taupe to a soft blue, the light hardwood floors and cream-colored couch brightening up the space. As I followed her into her kitchen, noticing the same flooring flowing throughout the downstairs, I stopped to look at the pictures she had hung on the wall. They were all scenic shots, and I had a feeling she was the photographer. She liked to mess around with the camera back in the day, often snapping unflattering pictures of me, mostly when I was goofing off with her, Mark, or Brooke.

"Do you want something to drink?"

"Some water would be great. Hey, did you take these?" Olivia glanced to where I pointed.

"A few years ago. Brooke and I went camping, and I couldn't pass up the view, or the sunset."

"They're really good. But you always had an eye for this."

"Thanks."

She released her hair from its messy bun and time slowed as her strands fell around her. Only seconds passed, but it felt like I was staring at her for hours. This woman was stunning, and I held the suspicion she didn't know how much, if at all. Even in her dirty overalls, she was sexy.

She handed me a glass of water before unzipping the front of her coveralls. I took my cue from her, figuring we were getting right down to it. I managed to unhook my belt with my free hand, but that was as far as I got when she scrunched her face.

"What are you doing?"

My hand stilled on my brown leather belt. "I thought we were getting undressed."

"I have to throw these in the washer. I have clothes on underneath."

"Oh." I failed at hiding the disappointment in my voice.

"You do know I wear something under these, right?"

"I do now." *A guy can fantasize.* I moved past her to check out the kitchen, and to get away from the awkwardness of me being a dumbass. "This looks amazing." The old cabinets had been a cherry color with dark countertops, and there had been a tiny island in the center which barely accommodated two people. She'd switched to white cabinets with a white-and-gray marble countertop, complete with a white subway tile arranged horizontally. The new island fit at least six chairs comfortably.

"My dad and Mark helped with the renovations. Saved me some coin, which I appreciated since I drained a decent amount of my savings on the down payment." Her eyes roved over the space, the pride on her face evident. "But it's mine."

"It's really nice. I'm assuming the main bedroom is now yours. I bet it's weird sleeping in a room where your parents probably did all sorts of dirty things."

"Oh my God. Stop it." She stepped out of her overalls and tossed them over the back of a chair, leaving her to stand in jeans and a plain pink T-shirt. "I painted the room, changed the carpet, and installed a new vanity and shower in the en suite bathroom. Any evidence of my parents has long since left."

Wanting to get down to it, I abruptly walked out of the kitchen, down the hall, and headed toward the stairwell, taking them two at a time. I remembered which room was her parents', now hers. She was hot on my heels, calling my name but I didn't stop until I entered her room. She was right. The room looked nothing like I remembered, which was good because being reminded of Mr. and Mrs. B wouldn't be such a good thing, especially not for what I had planned for their daughter.

"Which one of these has your underwear?" I pointed toward the large chest of drawers against the far wall.

"Why?"

"Because I want you to put on something sexy. It'll help. Trust me."

"First off, how do you know that?" I parted my lips to answer but she held up her finger. "Never mind. And secondly, I don't have anything sexy."

"That can't be true. Every woman has a few items." I looked back to the drawers. "Which one?"

On a sigh, she said, "Second one from the top."

Rooting through the drawer she indicated, there were piles of random pieces strewn about with no organization, which was odd because Olivia was a tidy person. Or at least she had been. One pair after another had either random sayings, such as Love or Superstar, were plain, or had polka dots on them like the ones she wore the other night. She'd told the truth. Not a single sexy item in the entire drawer.

"This is sad." A pair of her underwear hung from the tip of my finger, but she snatched them from me before I could toss them back inside the dresser.

"They're comfortable. And besides, who cares what kind of underwear I have? It's not like I keep them on when I have sex."

"They do make lingerie for women that's both comfortable *and* sexy."

"And you know this because you wear it a lot?"

"Very funny." I turned my wrist until my palm was face up. "Come on."

"Where are we going?"

"Take my hand and I'll tell you." I needed to touch her, even in the most innocent of ways. Thankfully, she didn't make me wait long before she accepted my offer. Tightening my grip, I pulled her from her bedroom, down the hall and descended the stairs.

"You still haven't told me where you're dragging me off to. I thought we were going to have sex. Isn't that the whole point of why you came over?"

"We will. But first, I have to rectify the sad situation that is your panty drawer."

She tried to dislodge her hand, but I held firm throughout the entire downstairs, and surprisingly she was quiet. But when we neared the front door, she finally opened her mouth.

"I need my purse."

"Why?"

"Because I don't know where we're going."

"Yes, you do."

Only a moment passed before she caught on. "I'm not going to Victoria's Secret with you."

"That's not where we're going."

"Where are you taking me?"

"Ollie." Her nickname flew from my mouth on a warning. "Grab your keys. You won't need anything else." When I opened the front door, she managed to yank her hand from mine, taking several steps to the side. She didn't utter another word, and even though I had an idea what ran through her mind, I didn't care. I wanted to run the errand and get back so I could spend hours trying to please her.

"It's getting late." Still, she didn't move. "I'll toss you over my shoulder if you don't move that sexy ass of yours." When Olivia remained frozen in place, I advanced a step and held my arms out, as if I were going to make good on my threat. She finally brushed past me and out the door, being sure to lock up before she descended the steps and headed toward my truck.

"I'm surprised you didn't insist on driving," I said, opening the passenger door for her.

"I don't know where we're going."

"You'll see."

"I'm not going in there, Luke. No way."

"You don't like their stuff?"

"I do. But I've browsed their website before, and they are *way* too expensive. Like a-hundred-and-forty-dollars-for-a-pair-of-underwear expensive.

"If it's on sale." The pinch of her brows amused me. "And so what?"

"I'm not spending that kind of money on something I can buy for like ten bucks."

"You're not spending anything. I'm buying."

"No, you're not."

"I am." I seized her wrist and gently hauled her toward the entrance to La Perla. After she glanced around at the other people walking by, she dipped her head, tugged her arm away from me, and stepped over the threshold to the expensive boutique.

A tall, blonde saleswoman dressed in a knee-length black dress approached us right away. Her smile was friendly. Perhaps a bit too friendly toward me, but thankfully she switched her attention to the irritated woman next to me.

"Can I help you find something?"

"No" was all Olivia said, turning back around to leave. Luckily, I snatched her hand before she disappeared on me. The last thing I wanted to do was expend unnecessary energy chasing her down, only to drag her back in here.

"Yes. We'd like to see what you have in…." My voice trailed off as I looked over at Olivia.

"What?"

"You have to give her your sizes."

With her lips clamped shut, I realized she was going to resist at every turn. I wasn't an expert on lingerie sizes, but I took a stab at it anyway.

"She's a 32 B and a large for the bottom." Olivia sucked in a quick breath, narrowing her eyes at me in either offense or annoyance. I couldn't readily say.

"A small B," she mumbled to the saleswoman.

"Okay. Let me gather a few things for you. In the meantime, if you see anything else you like, we can add it to the tray."

"The tray?" Olivia looked at me as the woman walked around the store, selecting various items.

"She'll put everything she chooses for you in a tray so you can pick what you want to try on."

"You've done this before I see."

"Only with one person. And it was years ago. She used to drag me to the store in New York whenever we visited." She didn't say as much, but the downturn of her mouth told me she didn't appreciate hearing about me buying lingerie for another woman. Or maybe I misread her. Either way, it would probably be smart not to reference the experience again.

She walked toward the back wall, trailing her fingers down a white silk robe before flipping the tag over. Her gasp was loud enough for me to hear twenty feet away. I'd been so busy enjoying the sway of her hips as she traveled the space, that her reaction startled me away from the image of bending her over the nearest chair.

With wide eyes and a slightly parted mouth, she shook her head with such vigor, I thought she was going to give herself a headache. I couldn't help it. I laughed, which only served to irritate her.

She glanced toward the exit, and I was on her before she fled, blocking her from leaving. Gripping her shoulders, I turned her around and ushered her toward the back of the store, where the dressing rooms were located. At least this way, I'd have more time to catch her if she tried to escape again.

"You can go into room two." The saleswoman had walked up behind us. "There's a few more items I think would be stunning, but you can start with these." She walked past us and placed the large tray on a table inside the dressing room she'd instructed us to enter. "You can go in there with her if you want." A smile tipped her lips but disappeared upon hearing Olivia's objection.

"Why would he go in with me?"

"Oh, I'm sorry. You're not together?"

I answered, "Yes," at the same time Olivia answered, "No."

The poor woman looked confused and slightly uncomfortable. "She's playing hard to get," I corrected.

The saleswoman left without another word, and when I turned my sights to my left, Olivia glared at me.

"You're not coming in here with me."

"I am."

"You're not," she argued.

"I am because you're going to need help, and my feedback. You can get whatever you feel good in, no questions asked, but if you're on the fence, there's no need to come out here each time. Besides, I figured you'd feel more comfortable not having perfect strangers see you in your underwear."

She appeared to give my points some consideration before she stepped aside, giving me adequate space to enter the dressing room.

15

OLIVIA

How had we gone from Luke rooting through my underwear drawer like he was searching for lost treasure, to standing in the dressing room of one of the most expensive lingerie shops?

Speaking of dressing rooms, this one was larger than my childhood bedroom, complete with flattering lighting, two chairs with a table in between, and mirrors lining each wall. There was even a pair of open-toed heels in my size.

"What do you want to try on first?" He picked up a sheer, red lacy thong, turning it for inspection. Not that there was much to examine. The scrap of expensive material wouldn't cover much at all. But I supposed that was the point.

I snatched it out of his hand. "If you're making me do this, I'll choose what I want to try on." To drive home my point, I tossed the underwear back onto the pile of items, picking one similar to the red one, only these were black. And the lace detailing was more intricate, although it exposed as much as the one he'd chosen. Placing the item to the side, I kicked off my shoes and socks. Next it was my jeans, but when I'd unzipped them and started to shimmy them down, I asked, "Can you turn around?"

"Why?"

"Because I need some privacy."

Luke barely gave my request a thought before he said, "No." He leaned back in his seat, spread his legs, as guys did, and rested his hands on the arms of the seat. "Get on with it, Ollie. We don't have all night. Remember what we have to get to once we're done here."

"Are you ever going to stop calling me that?" I hated to admit it, but the more he used my nickname, the less it aggravated me. But I'd never divulge that information.

"I'm not planning on it."

After a full ten seconds of an intense stare down, I huffed out my frustration and peeled my jeans off. Afterward, I stalled as to what to take off next.

His expression deadpanned, and I hated that I couldn't read him. Was he bored already? He was the one who dragged me here, and I hadn't even tried anything on yet.

"Shirt."

"Excuse me?"

"Take off your shirt. And lose the bra as well." I hesitated, but I wasn't sure why. The man had seen me naked, had fucked me two ways to Sunday, and had his mouth on almost every part of me. Why a bout of shyness crept in now was beyond me. "Now." The gruffness of his tone sent a shiver through me, and mixed with the serious look on his face, I almost threw myself into his lap.

Giving him my back, a pointless act because there were mirrors everywhere I turned, I gripped the hem of my T-shirt and raised it up my body until the material cleared my head, tossing it to the floor to join my discarded jeans. Next came my bra.

"It certainly is," he said, and I had no idea what he referred to until it dawned on me that I wore the underwear with *Juicy* printed across the ass.

I ignored his comment, spun back around, and picked up the black pair I'd initially selected. "Do I leave mine on while I try them?" I'd never tried on underwear before, so this was all new to me.

"You either leave yours on or they have disposable ones you can put on under the black ones." He pointed toward the corner at the blue packages of panties shelved together. There were all different styles, depending on what someone needed. Thongs, hipsters, bikinis, etc. As I tore into the package, he stopped me. "Better yet, take yours off and put the black ones on. You're getting them regardless. I just want to see what they look like."

"What if they don't fit?"

"They will."

"How can you be so—"

"Do it." Normally, I'd refuse on principle alone, but for some reason I complied, hooking my thumbs into the waistband and slowly dragging them down my legs, kicking them off to join the rest of my clothing.

I stood before him completely nude. The way his gaze drifted over me made my core ache, the wave of lust flashing behind his eyes almost stealing my breath.

Luke reached for the black thong before I could, leaned down, and tapped my ankle when I hadn't moved. With my hand on his shoulder, I inserted one foot after the other, holding still while he pulled them up, the pads of his fingers caressing my heated skin in the process. Because he was seated, he was eye level with my belly button, and when I turned to face the opposite way, my ass was practically in his face.

"What do you think?" I admired my reflection, twisting from side to side, before looking over my shoulder at him.

"Fuck," he growled, palming my right cheek before slapping it. Hard.

"Ow." I rubbed the affected area, refusing to admit his smack had excited me.

"You liked it," he teased, winking at me before standing and pushing me against the mirror behind me. "I know I did." He positioned my hand over his pants to feel his arousal.

"You really are an ass man."

"You have no idea." I wasn't sure if there was more to his comment besides the obvious, but I didn't have time to ask even if I wanted to. With his fingers gently wrapped around my throat, he leaned in until his mouth hovered over mine, my bare breasts brushing against his shirt. "I want you so much right now. I'd fuck you right here if I didn't think you'd scream."

"You're the noisy one out of us." I wasn't used to a guy being so vocal in bed. My ex barely made any noise when we had sex. Sometimes I didn't even know he'd finished until he climbed off me. Luke was the exact opposite. He made sure to let me know how much he enjoyed me.

"So far." He licked at my mouth but didn't kiss me. When he suddenly moved away from me altogether, he opened the dressing room door and called for the saleswoman.

"What are you doing?" I reached for my shirt, but he leaned into me, holding me in place with his body. "I'm practically naked." When we heard the click-clack of the woman's heels against the marbled floor, I struggled against him, but still I couldn't move.

"Did you need something?" she asked, peeking her head into the room. Even though Luke's body shielded mine, I had no doubt the mirrors lining the walls exposed parts of me.

"We'll take everything here. Throw in some robes and pajamas as well." He reached behind his back and pulled his wallet from his pocket. Everything was happening so fast, I barely had time to form an objection, let alone voice it. Once he handed her a card, he shifted us over a few steps so she could grab the tray with all the items in it. "She's going to wear the black lace thong home." If I could be any more embarrassed, I'd probably die.

"Good choice" was all she said, disappearing and leaving us alone once more.

"You're not buying all this stuff. I don't need it and I don't want it."

"I want you to have them."

"Why? So I can parade around for you like your other women did?" My question was as much of a shock to him as it was to me, my insecurity, or jealousy, clipping the end of each word.

"I told you I've only bought stuff from this store for one other woman, and she was the one dragging me there, not the other way around. Besides, it wasn't this location, and she didn't have any of the items you will."

"Is that supposed to make me feel special?" *Seriously, what is with these random questions?*

"You *are* special."

He loomed over me again, dipping to kiss the side of my neck. I shoved at his shoulders, but he refused to back up and give me an ounce of room. The air trapped between us turned stifling, and I barely managed to draw air into my lungs before he stole it when he smashed his mouth over mine.

His kiss was hungry, needy. He shoved his hand down the front of the panties he'd just purchased, dipping two fingers into my wet heat. His movements were hurried, his groans assaulting my eardrum, making me crave him. I rocked against his hand, swirling my tongue with his, and even though nothing would come of this, no physical reaction other than the ache between my legs serving to toy with me, I enjoyed every second of it.

Until there was a knock at the door.

"Everything is ready for you."

I was so lost to the feel of him, I never heard anyone

approach. But it was exactly what needed to happen. I shouldn't be gyrating against his skilled fingers, practically naked, in the dressing room of La Perla.

This time when I shoved him back, he retreated, taking his torturous hand with him.

"I have to get dressed." I pulled on my bra and T-shirt. "Buying me stuff wasn't part of the deal."

"Whatever I think is going to help, I'll do."

Luke sat back down in the chair, only this time he leaned forward instead of relaxing like he'd done only minutes before. With his forearms resting on the tops of his thighs, he dipped his head before looking back up at me. An expression crossed his face, but I couldn't decipher what it was before it was gone.

"How is lingerie going to help me come?" Working my jeans up my legs, I stuffed the pair of underwear I'd worn here into the front pocket.

"Can I have those?"

"No." I didn't need to ask what he referred to because his eyes were on my hip. Instead of insisting, he grinned. It was hard to be irritated with him for long because he always had that way about him that made me tolerate him more than I should. "You didn't answer my question."

"Which one?"

"I only asked you one. You don't remember?"

"That's two?"

"Two what?"

"Two questions. Which one do you want me to answer?"

"You're an ass," I grumbled. It was pointless to talk to him when all he wanted to do was rile me. I took two steps toward the door but didn't get far before he grabbed my wrist and pulled me back, hard enough to lose my balance and fall onto his lap. He swung my legs over the arm of the chair, pulling me so close, his breath fanned my cheek.

"Are you mad at me?" I didn't believe his question to be a serious one, the twitching of his cheek muscles a sure indicator.

"Yes."

"Why?"

"Because I don't want you buying things for me, especially stuff this expensive."

He toyed with my earlobe, dragging it through his teeth. "I can afford it." The corners of his eyes crinkled, a bit of his arrogance shining through.

Luke was a wealthy guy, but I didn't want anything from him, other than his body. I needed to keep things simple. *As if sleeping with him could ever be considered simple.*

"I don't care. We need to have boundaries."

"We do, though."

"No, we don't." I moved back so I could see more of his face, which wasn't a great plan because I instantly got lost in his eyes, wishing for things to be different between us. As the thought formed, it confused me. What exactly did I want to be different? I got to sleep with him, no strings attached. Although, it seemed to me he was trying to fasten me to him anyway he could. First, with his proposal to continue to help me out in exchange for being his date to his sister's wedding, and now with buying me lingerie. Was I making more of this than I should? That was yet to be determined.

I severed the eye contact and focused on his mouth, which was another mistake. When he licked his lips, his tongue staying to rest over his bottom one, mine parted. All I wanted was for him to kiss me again. It wasn't until he chuckled that I was shoved out of my haze of lust, clinging to a piece of it with the tips of my fingers.

I tried to get up, needing some distance from him in hopes of regaining some of my wits, but he grasped onto my hip.

"Just a few more minutes." His tone was soft, a hint of pleading entwined through his words.

"We have to go. I don't want anyone thinking we're doing anything in here. It's embarrassing." I wasn't sure if it was what I said or how I said it, but suddenly his eyes darkened.

"Fine." He pulled his hand away and I scrambled off his lap, but not before my ass ground against his crotch. "You're gonna pay for that one." Gone was the expression he just wore, replaced with a playful one.

"I didn't do it on purpose."

"Uh-huh. Sure."

Snatching my hand, he pulled me from the dressing room, adjusting the front of his pants as we walked toward the counter. I moved my arm back, trying to dislodge my hand from his for the hundredth time today, but the only thing I managed to accomplish was to make him tighten his grip.

This was exactly why we needed boundaries. Him holding my hand might seem like a simple gesture, one not to be read into, but for me, it blurred the lines.

And the last thing I wanted was to not have a clear eyeline on what it was he and I were doing.

I didn't need muddied waters.

I didn't want any confusion between us.

I had one goal in mind.

One which didn't include falling back in love with Luke Sorenson.

16

LUKE

The ride back to Olivia's house was silent. I didn't even turn on the radio for distraction, instead choosing to lose myself inside my own head, which probably wasn't the best thing to do.

We were headed to her place, to have sex. What I couldn't understand was why I was on edge. Was it because I knew if she didn't get off, neither would I? Or maybe it was because she continued to keep up some kind of guard around me. There were moments when I saw the old Olivia, from years back. My friend. The one girl who'd twisted me up so badly at one point, I almost threw away my scholarship to UCLA just to stay near her. But this version of her, the one with her arms crossed, staring out the window because she refused to look in my direction, would appear. She was hot and cold, and I couldn't seem to figure her out, no matter how hard I tried. Granted, I'd only been around her a few times since returning home from Miami, but our exchanges were enough to know I had my work cut out for me.

Pulling into her driveway, I cut the engine and hopped out, intending to walk around and open her door for her, but she

SIMPLY COMPLICATED | 111

was three steps away from her porch before I made it to the front of my truck.

"In a hurry to get naked?" I asked, lowering my voice only after looking around to see if we had an audience. Thankfully, we didn't.

She whipped around, her hair flying into her face with the movement. "Could you be any louder?"

"I guess we'll see soon enough."

She huffed, inserting her key into the lock before shoving the door open. I half expected her to slam the damn thing in my face, but she left it open a crack. After gathering the bags from La Perla, I walked into her house and straight up the stairs. I had no idea where she was, but I wasn't about to leave four bags of expensive lingerie anywhere but inside her bedroom. Besides, I might want her to model some more pieces for me. She'd only managed to try on one pair of underwear before I basically succumbed to my lust. I couldn't help it. Seeing her practically naked, even though I'd seen her in all her glory the other night, did something to me no other woman had managed to do.

Olivia was different.

She was special.

Life-changing, give-up-my-career type of special.

I'd held on to my feelings for her over the years, and even though I'd shoved them deep down, realizing I had no other choice, they were always there, on a slow simmer, only to be reignited the moment I saw her at McConley's. She didn't know this, but after overhearing, or eavesdropping, as she'd say, her conversation with Brooke, there was no way I'd ever let her leave with some random guy.

She was mine. She just didn't know it yet.

And as luck, or misfortune, would have it, depending on how one looked at it, she didn't come the first time we were together, prompting me to make the deal I had. My heart swelled when she accepted.

"There you are," she said, heading toward me, tossing her *Juicy* panties into her hamper.

"You could've given them to me as a souvenir."

"Ewww... no. Don't be a creeper, Luke." The faintest grin twisted her lips before it disappeared. "Besides, I would've thought you'd want these." She unbuttoned her jeans and slid the zipper down just enough so I could see the top of the black thong. A quick wiggle of her brows matched the shimmy of her hips as she pulled off her jeans and tossed them to the ground.

I swallowed the urge to pounce on her and worked to calm myself enough so I could draw out this encounter.

"Is there a matching bra in one of those bags?" she asked.

"Look who's on board now."

"There's no talking you out of something once you have your mind set. That much I remember about you." Off came her shirt, and her white satin bra. Her nipples were hard, and the quickening rise and fall of her chest told me what I wanted to know. She was excited. But did she feel sexy? Did she even know how beautiful and rare she was?

When she cleared her throat, a slight blush creeping over her skin, I dumped the bags on top of her bed and rooted through the items. Locating the matching piece, I handed it to her.

"Here you go."

The bra was almost as sexy as the thong, her pert nipples straining against the sheer lace. Probably not a practical piece to wear under clothing, but that wasn't the purpose right now.

Olivia looked down at herself, shifting her long hair to one side. "What do you think? Is it money well spent?" There was a blend of sarcasm and doubt weaved into her question.

"You look perfect."

She lifted her head, her eyes meeting mine only after she looked around the room. After another fleeting moment of unease on her part, she stood taller, her hands finding a home on her waist.

"How is wearing this going to help?"

I was in front of her before she could say another word, her short gasp at the suddenness of my movement just about undoing me. I was barely holding on to my restraint. Another sharp inhale of air, or a lick of her lips, or the come-hither look she didn't even know she wore, and she'd be underneath me.

"How do you feel wearing this?" I brushed the back of my hand over her nipple, and she shivered. "Do you feel sexy?"

"I like the way you look at me while I'm wearing it." Her teeth toyed with her bottom lip, her tongue peeking out to wet it afterward.

"That's not what I asked." I stepped behind her and positioned my hand at the nape of her neck, leaning into her, my mouth inches from her shoulder. "Do you feel sexy?"

"Yes." Her answer floated through the air on a whisper.

"Good." I circled my arm around her and pulled her into me, her ass pressing against my dick. I was so hard it hurt, and while I wanted to throw her onto the bed and have my way with her, this wasn't about me.

I moved my hands down her body and gripped her ass, loving the feel of her ample bottom. Giving her a squeeze, I rested my mouth near her ear and whispered, "When was the last time you came?"

"What?"

"I think you heard me just fine." My right hand moved to settle over her throat once more, and my other disappeared down the front of her panties, her hips bucking when I touched her clit. "Answer me."

"A mon... a month ago," she responded, tripping over her words.

I stopped teasing her and turned her around to face me. "A month ago?" My voice raised a bit with the question.

"So?"

"A month. As in thirty days?"

"When was the last time you did?" She appeared offended by my shock.

"This morning."

Her eyes darted to the front of my jeans before drifting back up to my face. "It better have been by your own hand. We have an agreement."

"Do you think so little of me that I'd break our deal, and so early on to boot?" Her narrowed eyes told me she was going to say something snarky, so I cut her off before a single word left her mouth. "Don't answer that. I told you I wouldn't sleep with anyone else while we're doing this, and I always keep my word."

"Just making sure."

"No need. Now get on the bed. We've got work to do."

17

OLIVIA

"Dammit. I thought we were close there."

Luke's effort was evident in the heave of his chest as he lay beside me, a sheen of sweat covering his skin, but the big finale never took place. Even though I was slightly disappointed it still hadn't happened, I thoroughly enjoyed every second. There was something to be said about a man who was solely focused on a woman's pleasure. Yes, that was the deal we'd both entered after the initial encounter, but he could've bailed after the first time.

Knowing Luke the way I did, though, he didn't back down from a challenge. He was competitive, annoyingly so at times. But his fierce edge would hopefully work in my favor.

"We?" I asked, turning my head in his direction.

"Yes. We. Remember, I'm not finishing either." He rolled onto his side and lay his arm over my belly. "Were you close at any point?"

I briefly lost my train of thought when his bottom lip disappeared between his teeth. Only when he dug his fingers into my side did I remember he asked me a question.

I didn't want to dash his hopes, but I wasn't going to lie to him either. What would be the point?

"No."

A crease formed between his brows, and he sighed.

"Don't get frustrated with me."

"I'm not frustrated with you at all." I tried to move his arm, but he wouldn't budge. When I made the attempt again, he pulled me closer, denying me an ounce of space. "Ollie, stop it. I'm serious. My little outburst has nothing to do with you. Well, it kind of does, but not in the way you think. I'm only trying to think of what else we can try for next time."

"Oh" was all I could say in response, silently berating myself for thinking the worst.

"Was there anything you've done before that brought you close?"

"By myself or with someone?"

He thought about my question for a moment. "With someone. Although, now I'm picturing you playing with yourself and I have to tell you, I'm getting hard again just thinking about it." And sure enough, his growing arousal pressed against my outer thigh.

"Calm down, big boy."

He positioned himself on top of me before I realized he'd even moved, nudging my legs apart so he could fit in between.

"Can you go again?"

"What's the point?" I tried to hide the defeat in my voice, but I failed.

"You know what the point is."

"I meant more for you. If it doesn't happen, you're going to be left without a release for the second time tonight."

"Then we'll be in the same boat." He lined himself up but didn't press any further. "Just the tip?" he asked, a wide grin stealing over his face.

But instead of answering, I grimaced when he shifted forward an inch, breaching my entrance. We'd gone at it vigorously for over a half hour, and now I was sore. Luke wasn't a small guy by any means, and even though there had been times he'd slowed things down, he'd also fucked me hard and fast.

I'd enjoyed him thoroughly, but now was left feeling as if maybe we should wait for another day. If I were being honest with myself, it wasn't purely for physical reasons. I simply didn't want to build up my hope for the second time tonight. Thinking even deeper on the subject, I wasn't sure if I was more concerned about him or me.

"Earth to Ollie." I'd been looking in his direction the entire time, but because I was lost inside my head, I'd looked right through him.

"How about we wait for next time?"

"Okay." He kissed me before rolling onto his back, much like he'd been minutes ago. "Do you mind if I stay over?"

"Yes."

"Yes, you mind? Or yes, I can stay over?"

"Yes, I mind."

"Oh." His voice was heavy with disappointment. "Can I ask why?"

I dared not to look at him for fear I'd cave. Having him sleeping next to me would only serve to confuse me. And if anything, I needed to have my head on straight whenever I was around him. I couldn't allow him to suck me back in like he'd done years ago. Making me crave his attention.

I didn't want a relationship with Luke. Once upon a time, I dreamed of the possibility, but he left and never looked back, showing me exactly what type of guy he really was. No, this arrangement was the furthest I was willing to take it with him.

Sex. Nothing else.

No complications. No other forms of intimacy other than what we'd agreed to.

"Because." I moved toward the edge of the bed, but he caught my wrist.

"That's all you're going to give me? Not an actual reason as to why you don't want me to stay over?"

Tugging back my arm proved futile. He wasn't going to let me go until I explained.

Deciding it was best to look him in the eye, I turned back toward him. "This is only sex. Nothing more. I don't want to complicate things by starting to blur the lines. You buying me lingerie was something I never should've allowed. But I'm stopping it there."

"You're stopping it there," he parroted, releasing my wrist and hopping off the bed. "Okay." His lips curved downward. "Good to know." He didn't say another word as he got dressed, his movements neither rushed nor lingering. His face was void of expression. Was he upset? Offended? Or did he understand and agree with me?

His shoes dangled from his fingers when he rounded the bed and stood beside me. "Can I kiss you goodnight, or would I be violating one of your rules?" A dash of hope danced behind his eyes, and while I wanted to throw myself into his arms, I didn't dare move from my position.

"I don't think that's a good idea either."

The brief silence dancing between us said more than words could at this point.

After raking his fingers through his hair, he dropped his arm to his side. For a second, I thought he was going to touch me, but he didn't. Did I want him to? Did I want him to ignore what I said and kiss me anyway?

I couldn't land safely on either answer, which was more frustrating than being able to choose.

Luke didn't utter another word as he walked out of my bedroom, leaving me to wonder if I'd just made a mistake.

18

OLIVIA

"Hey, sexy."

Brooke's voice registered before I saw her. I almost tripped over my feet from the shock of walking into my bedroom and finding my best friend there. She sat on my bed with the La Perla bags next to her, some of the items laid out in front of her.

"You scared me."

"Sorry."

"You couldn't let me know you were here?"

"Where's the fun in that? Besides, I didn't want to interrupt anything in case you had company in there."

"So, instead of 'interrupting me,'" I said, using air quotes, although, I wasn't sure it was warranted, "you wanted to surprise both of us had he been here? What if we were naked?"

"I would've gotten a front row seat." She twirled a pair of white panties in the air. All I could do was stare at her; my heart finally having slowed from being startled. "Oh relax, woman. I knew you were alone. Yours is the only vehicle in the driveway." Snatching my new underwear mid twirl, I tossed them back into one of the bags. "Did you win the lottery?"

"No. Why?" I knew where she was going with her soon-to-be interrogation.

"Because you don't spend money like this, and certainly not on this stuff. You've got at least ten thousand dollars' worth of lingerie. The sexiest thing I've ever known you to wear was a plain camisole, no bra."

"Maybe I wanted to splurge for once."

"Again… no. Besides, you're cheap."

"I'm not cheap. I'm financially smart."

She rolled her eyes. "Is this financially smart?" The rustling of the bags amplified her question. I tried to think of something else to say to get her off topic, but before I could, her eyes widened, and her mouth parted. Brooke wasn't dumb. I was surprised it took her this long to put it together. "Luke bought these for you, didn't he?" Her finger was pointed right at me, continuing to speak even before giving me a chance to confirm or lie or deflect. The last two options would be pointless, however. "He did. Don't even try and deny it."

"He said it would help."

"Oh, I'm sure he did." Her thought process had been my initial route as well. "Too bad we're not the same size. I'd borrow some of these."

"You'd borrow my underwear? I love you, but not that much."

"Borrow. Take. Same thing."

Brooke was a few inches taller than me, had much bigger boobs, and a smaller butt. I was envious of her shape, but she'd often tell me she was envious of mine. I supposed one always wanted what they didn't have.

Tightening the towel around me, I opened my dresser drawer, pulling out a pair of underwear to go under my pajamas.

"Do you really think all of that cost ten thousand dollars?" I asked, waving my finger in the direction of the lingerie bags.

"At least."

I groaned, knowing I shouldn't have let him buy me all of it. A matching set would've been more than enough. Why didn't I put up more of an argument when he handed his credit card to the saleswoman? *Because you were too busy being seduced by him.*

"I should return all of it."

"Don't you dare. Besides, the guy can afford it. I doubt this was even a drop in the bucket for him."

"Because he's wealthy, I should take advantage?"

"That's not what I meant at all. Obviously, he wanted to buy you this stuff. Let him. Keep it. Besides, someone is smitten."

"I am not. I'm only using him."

"I wasn't talking about you, Liv." Brooke tapped her finger against her lips. "Tell me you don't realize Luke wants you."

"He's got me. Well, until...." My words trailed off because she knew what came after *until.* "And he's not smitten with me. He's just a guy who gets to have sex. A lot of sex. Countless positions in one session kind of sex." Luke's image popped into my head, and on some miniscule level I felt like I was betraying him. The thought was odd, as Brooke was my best friend, and Luke wasn't even my friend. Once he had been. He'd meant even more to me, but the problem was, it was only ever one-sided.

"You like him," she blurted, grinning from ear to ear.

"I do not."

"You do. But he likes you too, so what's the problem?"

"The problem is..." I released breath after breath, attempting to form a coherent thought. But the only thing I came up with as a retort was more denial. "I don't like him. I'm just using him. You know this."

"Speaking of being used and abused, where is he?"

"I don't know. I haven't heard from him today." I took a seat next to Brooke. "He might be upset with me."

"For what reason?"

"He asked if he could stay over last night, and I told him it wasn't a good idea. I didn't want to blur any lines. It's easier if we keep this strictly sexual. Nothing more."

"That was harsh."

Ignoring her comment, I kept talking. "He also asked if he could give me a kiss goodnight." I scrunched my face, giving her the answer to her next question, but she asked anyway.

"You told him no?" I nodded. "Olivia! What is wrong with you? You kiss while you're having sex, right?" Another nod from me. "What would be the big deal if you kissed him goodbye? I'm lost here."

"It's different. It's too familiar, if that makes sense."

"Not a lick."

As she continued to defend Luke, consequently vilifying me in the process, I got upset, storming off into the bathroom to change into my pajamas. When I reentered the bedroom, I plopped down on the bed beside her, falling to my back and throwing my arm over my face. Why did I feel like I'd done something wrong?

Deciding not to blame myself for a decision I made in the moment, one I was sticking by, I tried to explain it in a way Brooke might understand, all while keeping my eyes closed. I didn't want to have to witness her eye rolling, or one of the hundred faces she was sure to make at me.

"Men do this stuff all the time to women. Sex with no expectations. No strings attached. However you want to put it."

"But Luke is not all men. He's... Luke. Our friend. You know him."

"All too well."

"I'm not talking about *that*."

"Neither am I."

She smacked my leg, and not gently either. "Okay, spill it. What's with the whole 'I can't stand him' crap?"

"I don't want to get into it." Delving into the past was the last thing I wanted to do.

"Maybe if you told me, I could convince you that whatever happened wasn't as bad as you remember."

"That's exactly why I don't want to get into it."

"Come on, Liv. If you tell me, I'll stop being mad at you for keeping something from me. We made a pact in second grade to always tell each other everything. I've kept my end of the deal. Now it's your turn."

Her tone softened the longer she spoke, and I couldn't help but smile at the memory of two seven-year-old girls, vowing to share all life's secrets with the other. But she was right. Brooke told me everything, sometimes too much. It was only fair I clue her in on what happened in Luke's bedroom ten years ago.

So, I did, reliving the memory as I told her every single detail.

19

LUKE

I was man enough to admit that after Olivia basically kicked me out of her house, refusing to kiss me goodbye, my ego had been severely bruised. She had every right to enforce boundaries, but it didn't stop my self-esteem from taking a hit. I'd never asked to spend the night after sex with anyone before. The woman was always the one asking me to stay.

But after giving what she'd said more thought, I calmed down some. I didn't appreciate the delivery, or the way she looked partially horrified when I'd asked to stay over, but the message was clear.

She wanted to keep things between us strictly focused on the deal we'd made. And while I accepted our arrangement for what it was, a guy trying to help a woman out, nothing more, nothing less, I thought perhaps there was a chance our relationship could turn into something more. Not that we were in a relationship, per se, but I thought, at the very least, we could get back to being the friends we'd been before I moved away.

I'd had no communication with Olivia since the other night, needing the time to consider whether it was a good idea to continue as we had been. It was a stupid thought to even contemplate breaking our deal because what guy in his right mind would do so? The woman was gorgeous, and I was sleeping with her, just not in the same sense as I'd asked for the last time I'd been there.

My thoughts were all over the place, and if I didn't get a handle on them before I reached my destination, I feared I'd end up doing or saying something I'd soon regret. What that could be, I didn't have a clue, but the moment I saw her face, I was scared I would have a knee-jerk reaction, especially if she acted a certain way or said something I didn't appreciate.

A text to let her know I was coming would've been smart, but when it came to Olivia, I didn't always have my wits about me.

Turning into the parking lot of Brighton's Automotive, her Jeep Wrangler was parked off to the side of the building. Mark's Silverado and Mr. B's Grand Cherokee were housed in the spaces next to her vehicle. *Great, they're all here.* But what had I expected? It was two in the afternoon on a Thursday. Of course, they'd all be at work. And the only reason I wasn't at practice was because we had an early one today. Something about Coach having an appointment he couldn't miss.

After killing the engine, I hopped out of my truck and walked straight into the garage. I'd spent many hours here back in the day, Mr. B teaching me and Mark simple tasks, such as changing the oil, as well as a tire. I'd even helped to switch out the brakes on a Honda once. But that was as far as my automotive knowledge went.

After I left for college, I'd gotten too busy to look under the hood of any of my vehicles, and as time passed, I had enough money I could just hire someone else to do repairs. But because I never kept a vehicle longer than three years, the only issues I ran into were replacing wear and tear items. In fact, the truck I pulled up in was only six months old, the same model Mark had, only much newer.

"Hey, Luke," Mr. B called out, tossing a tattered oil rag over his shoulder. "What brings you by?"

Having a cover story for my sudden appearance would've been smart, but I blamed Olivia for having me all twisted up. So I said the first thing I could think of, which was a lie.

"My truck's making a rattling noise. I thought if you guys had any time today, you could check it out for me."

"Sure. Let me take a look." I handed him my keys, going into a little bit more detail about the issue, berating myself for making the man waste his time. While he was busy investigating a fake noise, taking my truck for a quick ride, I scoured the area for any signs of Olivia, but she wasn't in the garage. Mark, however, had just walked in from the office.

"Hey. What's up?" He clapped me on the shoulder, standing directly in front of me, but I struggled to give him my full attention, continuing to look for his sister, but trying not to make it obvious.

When we were younger, Mark had told me he appreciated how I looked out for her like he did. He loved that Olivia basically had two older brothers to protect her, and he was grateful he had someone else in his corner in case he had to teach a guy a lesson for messing with her. He was super protective over her when they were kids, and I wondered if his protectiveness had waned or gotten worse with time. I'd think he'd become more lax, seeing as how she was a grown woman now, but Mark was always steadfast about family and loyalty. Good qualities to have for sure, but things that might get in my way.

"Luke?" Mark's voice tore me away from my inner ramblings.

"Sorry. I'm thinking about the upcoming game. What did you say?"

"I asked why you were here?"

"Oh." I took a breath, hating that I was going to lie to my

friend like I did his father. "My truck is making some kind of noise. Your dad took it for a ride to check it out."

"We had a cancellation today, so we'll have time to give it a more thorough look once he gets back."

"Appreciate it."

"You can hang out in the office if you want. Olivia put on a pot of coffee recently. Help yourself."

Without trying to look too eager, I asked, "She's here too?"

He looked at me oddly. "She works here. Remember?"

"Oh, yeah." I played it off like nothing, but the way his eyes studied me made me uneasy. Perhaps I read too much into his expression, the knowledge that his sister and I were *involved* making me see things that might not be there. I left him in the garage and waltzed into the office. I was in the middle of pouring a cup of coffee when Olivia entered, wiping her hands with a paper towel before tossing it into the garbage.

"Hi," she said, looking me up and down before focusing on my face. I was dressed in jeans and a plain white tee, but her perusal of me made me want to strip naked, do the same to her, and bend her over the desk she leaned against.

I glanced toward the garage before speaking, making sure no one was around. "We good?"

A quick tip of her head was all the response I needed.

Placing my coffee on the table beside me, I took several steps toward her, near enough to satisfy my need to be closer, but far away enough to be considered inconspicuous in case her dad or brother walked in.

"Are we getting together later?" I asked, eager for her to say yes.

"We can. But I have to pick up my mom from work at seven. I can meet you at my house at eight."

"That works." I didn't move from my spot, and neither did she, and for several moments we stared at each other. Even dressed in her overalls, her hair twisted up and secured on top of her head, no makeup, and a tiny smudge of dirt near her temple, she was still gorgeous.

Parting my lips to ask her if there was anything she wanted to try that we hadn't so far, I didn't get a single word out before she spoke.

"Did you come here just to ask me about hooking up tonight?" I thought she looked excited at the prospect, but again, I could be seeing something that wasn't there—my own hopefulness mirrored falsely back at me.

I had a choice. I could tell her the truth, risking she'd be pissed because I was wasting her dad's time by looking at my truck unnecessarily, or I could stick to what I'd told Mark and Mr. B. The latter seemed to be the best choice. Worst case, they spent a few minutes giving it a thorough look over and didn't find anything wrong. Although, that would be best case for me seeing as how the truck was new.

"My truck is making a rattling sound. Your dad is looking at it." As if on cue, Mr. B pulled into the lot, hopping out and heading straight for Mark, who pointed to the office and right at me. As soon as their dad walked in, he shook his head, the dour look on his face confusing me. I'd made up the issue with my vehicle, so why was he looking at me as if he had bad news?

"I didn't hear a rattling noise, but there is a recall on the brake caliper bolts."

"Oh. I had no idea."

"No big deal. Olivia can put it up on the lift and take a look. I would but I need to replace Ella's brakes and tires." He glanced at his daughter. "You're still able to pick her up later, right?"

"Yes." She held out her hand and her father placed my keys in her palm. Her eyes were on me when she said, "If you have somewhere to go, you can take my Jeep until I'm done. Or you can wait here. Your choice."

"I'll wait." What I wanted to tell her was that I wanted to watch her work, even if she was only going to be inspecting my truck and not doing any actual repairs to it. Although, I shouldn't speak too soon. I didn't even know about the recall.

"Suit yourself," she said, exiting the office.

I'd waited for a total of three minutes and twenty-two seconds before I made my way into the garage, standing a foot from where Olivia inspected my truck. She briefly made eye contact with me, but otherwise her full attention was on what she needed to do. After another five minutes had passed, and she still hadn't said a word, I stepped closer, standing directly behind her as she searched for a tool she needed.

"I can't wait to get you naked later." The proximity of our bodies wasn't appropriate, and if her brother or dad looked over here, they would most likely start to think something, but in that moment, I couldn't find the energy to care.

"Stop it," she whispered through gritted teeth, slapping my hand away when I palmed her ass cheek.

"Watching you work is turning me on." I seized her hand when she tried to smack me again and placed it over my arousal. "See. I'm so hard right now."

She yanked her arm back and continued to search through the mess of metal objects on the rolling cart. Only when she turned to the side was I able to see the faintest smile on her lips.

"You better step back. I wouldn't want you to get hurt."

As it turned out, there was nothing wrong with my truck. The bolts she'd inspected were good. I should've been happy with the news, but all I kept dwelling on was her comment.

You better step back. I wouldn't want you to get hurt.

Olivia had no idea how profound her statement was, and I decided on the ride home, after having repeated the words a hundred times to myself, to be like her.

To treat our arrangement as nothing more than what it was.

Purely sexual.

Me helping her out.

Nothing more.

OLIVIA

Strolling through the lobby of Mountain View Medical Center, all I could think about was Luke, even though I tried hard not to. But the man had ingrained himself into my brain, and I couldn't help but picture his face or remember how much I loved kissing him. Not to mention the amazing sex. And even though I hadn't been able to orgasm yet, I thoroughly enjoyed myself whenever we got down and dirty. I admired him taking a stance, not coming until I did, but I honestly didn't know how he ever lasted as long as he did without losing control and just saying fuck it. Every pun intended.

There was an older couple waiting for the elevator when I rounded the corner. I entered with them, pressing the button for the fifth floor.

My mom was an obstetrics nurse, had been since before my brother and I were born. After taking a year off after having each of us, she went back to work. My dad told her she didn't have to because the garage was lucrative, still was to this day, but she loved her job.

The chime of the car sounded right before the doors parted, and as I walked down the long hallway, taking my first left, I saw my mom up ahead. She was walking toward the nurses' station desk, chatting away with a doctor in a mid-length white coat. The man was handsome, like he was an actor pretending to be a doctor kind of handsome.

"Olivia, honey. You could have just called me. You didn't have to come all the way up here."

"My phone died."

It was like she didn't even hear me, snatching my hand once I was close enough and pulling me next to her.

"But now that you're here, I'd like you to meet someone." *Oh Lord, here we go again.* The woman would never stop trying to set me up, even after the whole debacle with Doug, who turned out to like her and not me. Though, if anyone asked her, she'd say I was way off base, that I'd imagined the whole thing. "This is Derek Rozelle. He's a doctor." The smile on her face couldn't get any bigger, and while I was embarrassed by another one of her antics, I had to admit I didn't mind meeting this guy.

"I can tell by the coat, Mom." I extended my hand and he reciprocated, the warmth of his touch soothing the eruption of nervousness swirling in my belly.

"Ella has told me a lot about you, Olivia." His voice had a seductive rasp to it, and I wondered how many women fell over themselves merely to hear him talk.

"I'm sorry about that."

"I'm not," he responded, a dimple in his right cheek appearing. He looked me up and down, his gaze lingering on my mouth for several seconds before making eye contact again. "I hear you're a mechanic. That's a different choice in profession."

Whatever vibes I'd been feeling from this guy were crushed the second he vomited those last six words.

"What does that mean?" Hiding the irritation in my voice proved futile. I dealt with enough misogyny from the customers at work, I didn't need to deal with it from someone who probably had a God complex, no matter how good-looking he might be.

"Olivia." Whenever my mom whisper-shouted my name, I knew she wasn't pleased with me. But right now, I didn't care.

Derek shifted from one foot to the other. "I'm sorry. I didn't mean any offense. I only meant there aren't a lot of female mechanics out there. I would've thought you'd go into something more…."

"More what? More suited for women?" Before I realized it, my hands were on my hips and my head tilted to the left. He opened and closed his mouth several times, looking back to my mother. I had enough on my mind with Luke, I didn't need to stand here and listen to some jerk berate my choice of occupation. Turning my focus to the woman who'd done another stellar job of picking the wrong guy for me, I said, "I'll be out front."

I immediately turned and walked away, but I didn't make it ten steps before there was a hand on my elbow. When I looked, I saw Dr. Asshat was the person connected to said hand.

"I'm sorry. I didn't mean for what I said to come out the way it did. I was trying to say I would've thought you'd be happier doing another job."

Was he serious?

I yanked my arm back, and his fell to his side. His brows furrowed because he still didn't get it. He was being rude, and he didn't even realize it. His looks and the prestige he got as a doctor may excuse his behavior with other people, but I refused to stand here and be insulted to my face.

"Obviously, my mom doesn't know you at all if she thought this would be a good set up." Every word I spoke was painted with contempt. "And for your information, I love my job. And I'm damn good at it. Better than anyone else you know." Was that a wide net I cast? Sure, but I wasn't taking it back.

"I'm sure you deal with a lot of assholes treating you less

than because they're not used to seeing a female mechanic." His cheeks puffed up right before he blew out a breath. "That was the point I was trying to get across. I think it's cool you work in a garage. I can barely change my oil."

"Let me guess. You have a Benz or a BMW." My defensiveness slowly waned, his explanation working to erase some of my annoyance.

"BMW. Is it that obvious?"

"Yup." A shadow of a smile found its way on to my mouth. His stare bounced from my eyes to my lips and back again. More than once.

"This was all a misunderstanding. Let me make it up to you. I have a break. Join me for a cup of coffee while Ella finishes up."

I looked around him and saw her staring at us, smashing her hands together like she was praying.

"Okay. But if you make another offhanded comment, you'll be wearing that coffee."

He put his hand over his heart. "I promise not to sound stupid again."

He fell into step beside me as we walked toward the other end of the long hallway. He led me to a small breakroom, ushering me inside after he assured me I was allowed.

There were two other women sitting at one of the tables. They were all smiles when he entered, but when their gazes landed on me, their expressions flattened.

Derek was handsome, so their reaction to him wasn't surprising. And while I had no plans to see him after this encounter, I could appreciate a good-looking man. I didn't have butterflies in my belly like I did whenever I saw Luke, something I'd never admit to anyone, but this guy was nice to look at.

Over the course of the next half hour, I found out he'd moved here to Vegas from Colorado, that he was in his second year of residency, and that he wanted to specialize in cardiovascular. He had a dog named Bo, two sisters, one older and one younger, and his parents bragged about him every chance they got, most times embarrassing him. He asked me about my life, and compared to his, I didn't have much to offer other than what I did for a living and that I was close to my family. I left out the part about having sex with a famous soccer player because I didn't think that would go over too well.

Peeking at my watch, I was surprised how the time had flown by.

"I should be going." I moved to stand, and Derek did as well.

"I'd love to do this again sometime soon. Maybe dinner?"

In that moment, a wave of guilt washed over me, and it had everything to do with Luke. No, we weren't dating, and we'd agreed not to sleep with anyone else while we were *involved*, but the thought of a future meetup with Derek didn't sit right. But I didn't want to miss out on the opportunity to get to know the good doctor a little better. There was no harm in having dinner, right? Besides, this thing with Luke and I would never go anywhere past where we were and what we were doing. The internal back and forth was dizzying, and it wasn't until Derek touched my arm that I made a decision.

"Dinner would be nice." Short and simple, leaving room for future possibilities.

"My schedule is a little crazy, but can I call you once I know I'll have a night free?"

After exchanging numbers, he leaned in and kissed my cheek. When he stepped back, I saw my mom hovering in the doorway, smiling like she'd won the lottery. And I supposed setting her daughter up with a doctor would qualify.

***

When I pulled into my driveway, Luke was waiting for me. I was late in meeting him. Again. This wasn't like me. If anything,

I was usually early, but my coffee date with Derek had not only been unplanned but had gone on longer than I'd anticipated once we sat down.

"Sorry." I rushed past him to open the front door. "My mom had some things to finish up at work." What I'd divulged hadn't been a complete fabrication.

He didn't say a word as he followed me inside, heading straight for the stairs. His shirt was off before he reached the top, and his shoes were kicked off in the middle of the hallway.

Someone's eager to get started.

When I finally entered my bedroom, he was in the process of taking off the rest of his clothes. Once he was fully nude, he stalked toward me. Not a "hello," or a "how are you" left his lips before he backed me against the nearest wall. His mouth covered mine, his kiss aggressive, demanding, not at all gentle. Which normally I wouldn't mind, especially during the foreplay portion of our trysts, but there was something off with him. I couldn't pinpoint what it was, and he never allowed me any time to try and figure it out before he was tearing at my clothes.

My shirt was on the ground seconds later, the button to my jeans being popped open right before he yanked down my zipper. He sucked at my neck, dragging the material down my legs. When he stopped to look at the panties I had on, he frowned. Did he expect me to wear the stuff he bought me to work?

He tore my panties apart before I realized he even had a hold of the blue cotton material. I teetered between liking the aggressiveness, and being pissed he'd ruined a pair of my underwear.

Gripping the underneath of my backside, he raised me up his body. I locked my legs around his waist without instruction and returned his hungry kiss, our tongues dancing wildly together.

Typically, by this point, Luke would have said ten different dirty things to me, all of which would've turned me on even more, but so far, he hadn't uttered a single word. He growled, made several noises, which I assumed were some variations of enjoyment, but not a single syllable was spoken.

Granted, I hadn't said anything other than voicing my apology at being late and the half-truth as to why.

When he unhooked my ankles and tossed me onto the bed, looming near the edge, he gripped himself and stroked from base to tip. His stare was filled with desire, but his expression confused me. I'd come to enjoy the quick arch of his brow and the sexy smirk that usually appeared right before he licked his lips. But standing before me, he appeared to be indifferent. When he showed up at the garage earlier today, he'd asked me if we were good. I said yes, but his current actions were indicative of him not sharing the sentiment.

Was he getting bored with our arrangement? Frustrated I hadn't been able to orgasm yet? Did he want to end things with me but didn't know how to? Or did he want to keep having sex just for the sake of it?

So many questions.

Luke grabbed my ankles, and he was either going to flip me onto my stomach or pull me toward the edge of the bed. I moved my legs, or at least I tried to.

"What's wrong with you?" I finally blurted, having had enough of his version of the silent treatment. His hold on me intensified, and from the bulge of his biceps, he was still set to do whatever he had planned before I asked my question. "Luke." His name came out as both a warning and a question.

"Nothing's wrong." His chest expanded on a quick inhale. Instead of making another move like I thought he would, he stood there and stared at me, and I didn't like the way his scrutiny made me feel. Like he was judging me. But for what I couldn't figure out.

This time when I tried to dislodge his hands from around

my ankles, he released me. "Something's wrong. You haven't said two words to me."

"Nothing's wrong is two words." There was a glimmer of the Luke I knew, but he disappeared when he hardened his expression. "Are we going to do this or not?" The tone he used pissed me off, like I was nothing more than a warm body for him to stick his dick in.

"Seriously, what's the matter with you? Why are you acting all cold?" I wanted to cover up, but didn't want to appear self-conscious. Not when we were possibly going to be arguing.

"You said you wanted to keep this strictly sexual. Tight boundaries. That's what I'm doing."

I should've known what I'd said to him would come back to bite me, and after talking to Brooke about it, I understood Luke had probably been offended. Hell, I didn't need my best friend to point out that fact, I'd seen it written all over his face before he stormed out. Stormed out was a bit of a reach, but he didn't linger behind either.

"But you seem like you're mad at me." The thought he could be didn't sit well, and despite wanting to keep an emotional distance from him, I didn't want him to be detached. And if I thought he wasn't going to give his best effort, we should stop right now.

"I'm not." In a surprising move, he laid down beside me.

"I think you're lying."

"Maybe a little."

Rolling onto my side, I rested my hand on his chest, loving the feel of him beneath my fingers. Tracing a circle around his nipple, he flinched, his faint smiling mirroring my own.

"I shouldn't have said what I did the other night. Yes, I need there to be some boundaries, but that doesn't mean we can't talk about stuff. We're friends, right?"

Now it was his turn to roll toward me, my hand falling away to rest between us. "Are we? Because sometimes you act like you truly don't like me. Like down to your soul, don't care for me as a person."

"That's not true. I've… I've just been cautious around you."

"I'm not going to hurt you." He tucked a strand of my hair behind my ear, his fingers trailing down the side of my face. I returned his gaze and lost myself in his gorgeous eyes.

I believed that *he* believed what he said to be true, but I couldn't go there with him again. I should spill everything, delve into how upset I'd been years ago, how my embarrassment had morphed into disbelief, and deep-seated anger. But I didn't want to ruin the moment, so I didn't say anything on the subject.

Moments of silence lingered, and for the first time since meeting back up with him, a sense of ease enveloped me.

"How was practice?"

He smiled at the proverbial olive branch I extended, but instead of answering, he rolled on top of me. "I don't want to talk about that."

"What do you want to talk about?" I breathlessly asked, squirming when he kissed the sensitive spot near my earlobe.

"I want to talk about your tits." A sliver of pain erupted when he pinched my nipple. "I love how they bounce when I'm fucking you."

"They're not big enough to bounce," I countered. "And besides, don't use that word. It's so crass."

"Bounce?" The corners of his mouth twitched.

"Tits."

"What's wrong with tits?"

"I told you, it's crass."

"Then I'm assuming you don't like the word cunt?"

"Ugh! No." My corresponding expression when I emphatically answered made him chuckle.

"I don't use the word during everyday conversation, but during sex I think it's hot." He lowered his mouth to my ear.

"Like if I said, 'I can't wait to bury my tongue in your cunt,' that would turn you off?"

The rasp of his voice deepened when he posed his question, and I hated to admit it, but I didn't mind the word when he used it like that.

"Okay, during sex it's all right." I wriggled beneath him when he stuck his tongue in my ear, the action ticklish, yet a turn on.

"Told you." Luke pushed my legs apart as he pulled back to look at me. "What were you thinking about the last time you came?"

"What?" I stalled for time and he caught on.

"You heard me just fine. Tell me. I promise I won't judge you. If you only knew what I thought about when I...." He stopped speaking, scrunching his face as if I'd guess at his deepest, darkest fantasies. "This isn't about me."

"I think it should be."

"Nope. Give me your answer."

"Or what?"

He briefly looked over my head toward the window, biting his lip before shrugging.

"I can't think of a consequence right now. Especially not when you're gyrating against me."

I'd been slowly moving my hips underneath him without even realizing. It was like my body separated from my mind and had its own agenda. One I was completely on board with.

Silently bouncing between telling him or not, I decided to be honest.

"You."

"Me, what?"

"The last time I had an orgasm, I was thinking about you."

His eyebrows nearly hit his hairline before pinching together. "But you said it's been a month, and we haven't been having sex nearly that long." My silence filled in the blank for him. "Ohhhh." It took him a total of six seconds to lose the cocky grin before he pried his lips apart again. "If you came while thinking about me, I'm unsure why you can't do it with me here in person. What was I doing to you?"

In my flustered state, wanting to keep my thoughts private, I made a fluttering noise with my lips and cleared my throat twice. *No subtlety whatsoever.*

He knew I was lying when I replied, "Nothing out of the ordinary. Just stuff we've been doing," but he didn't call me out on it. "Maybe fantasies are better than reality?"

"Ouch," he said with a laugh to let me know he wasn't entirely offended.

"That came out wrong." The press of his lips to mine gifted me a pass for my thoughtlessness.

"I've fantasized about fucking you countless times over the years, but I can tell you without a doubt the real thing is so much better."

He's thought about me these past ten years?

I refused to travel down that road, so instead, I wrapped my legs around him and weaved my fingers through his thick hair.

"Prove it."

21

LUKE

I wouldn't consider tonight a failure. Sure, Olivia still hadn't orgasmed, but she'd admitted we were friends, which was a big step for her, considering there were times she didn't seem to like me.

"I'll think of something different for next time," I said, pulling my shirt over my head before fastening my belt. Ideas as to what to try were slowly being checked off, none of them proving fruitful as of yet.

"I will too." She was on her back stretched out, her skin tinged pink from her own exertion. The woman tried as hard as I did, but for some reason she hadn't been able to get there. Yet.

"We'll figure it out together." I sat on the side of her bed, pulling my shoes on when her phone dinged from an incoming text. It was followed by another, and another. "Someone sure wants you."

"Can you grab that for me? It's probably Brooke."

"Sure." I crossed the room and disconnected her cell from the charger. On the lock screen I saw the texts were indeed from her best friend, but as I walked back toward her, another text came through, this time from someone named Derek. The only way I could see what he typed was if I opened her phone, and I doubted she'd appreciate my intrusiveness. But I needed to know who this guy was contacting her. "Who's Derek?" I barely disguised my raging jealousy when I asked the question. The widening of her eyes made my heart beat faster, emphasizing this guy was someone I might need to be worried about.

"Someone my mom wanted me to meet." She held out her hand waiting for me to give her the phone.

"And did you?"

"Did I what?"

"Meet him?" The device slipped from my fingers and fell to the bed next to her. She didn't answer, but she didn't unlock her screen to read his message either. "Olivia?"

"Yes, I did."

"When?" A silent reminder to remember to breathe would be good right about now.

"Earlier."

"Tonight?" The inflection in my voice surprised both of us.

"Yes, all right." She hopped up and grabbed a short white satin robe from the back of her door, one of the items I'd bought her from La Perla. "I went to pick up my mom from work and he was standing there talking to her. She practically forced him on me."

"I bet." The erratic beat of my heart intensified. "Is he another tech?"

"He's a resident."

"He's a doctor?"

I had more money than I could ever spend in two lifetimes. I was famous, successful, and never had an issue getting attention from women. But standing here in front of Olivia, hearing about how her mother introduced her to a doctor, a man whom Olivia had obviously given her number to, a man who was now texting her, I became insecure. This was an odd feeling for me. And it was more than jealousy at this point.

"So?"

"So," I repeated, running my hand over the top of my hair. "You're not going to see him again, are you?"

"I was considering it."

"You're considering it," I whispered, more to myself than to her. "What about our deal? We agreed not to sleep with anyone else while we were still doing this." I motioned back and forth between us.

"Jesus, Luke. I'm not going to have sex with the guy. It's only dinner."

"Now it's dinner?"

"Why are you getting upset?" She had the nerve to ask me such a stupid question. How would she feel if some woman I'd just met texted me? She'd be pissed. "We said no sex with anyone else. We didn't say no dating."

"Technicalities."

She ignored my response. "You and I aren't dating. And who knows how long it'll be before...." Her words trailed off. "I don't want to miss out on meeting someone I might like."

My head screamed everything she'd said was justifiable, but my heart was another matter altogether. Not to mention the green-eyed monster begging to break free inside me. Weighing the outcome of the numerous responses I wanted to voice, I held my tongue, realizing things could go from awkward to detrimental in a matter of seconds. In the end, I acted like what was happening wasn't a big deal at all.

"I wouldn't want you to miss out either, Ollie. You have my blessing. Not that you need it." I turned to walk away, but she grabbed my arm before I reached the door, the sides of her robe parting enough I was reminded she was naked underneath. As if I could've forgotten.

"Are you mad?"

The Olivia from the other day wouldn't have asked me that question. And because I didn't want to ruin any progress we'd been able to make tonight, I leaned in and kissed her cheek, lingering longer than necessary.

"No. I'll talk to you later."

Today had been an extra grueling practice, and I was frustrated I hadn't been as focused as I needed to be. Not only had I gotten reamed out by Coach, again, but some of the other players gave me the side-eye. I was part of this team now and I needed to bring my A game, but all I could manage to do was perform like an amateur. Not like the player I knew I was. The player the team had paid for.

It'd been five days since I'd found out Olivia had met someone, and although neither of us brought it up again, this Derek guy, this doctor who was interested in the woman I'd been having sex with, was someone I needed to be worried about.

Once I was behind the wheel, I unlocked my screen and called her.

"Hey," she answered, sounding out of breath. All sorts of torrid images popped into my head, but I dismissed them all, fully aware she was at work.

"You okay?"

"I just got done unloading a shipment of parts we'd been waiting on. I'm so out of shape."

"Maybe we'll have to incorporate some acrobatics into our sessions."

Olivia still hadn't been able to orgasm, and I was running out of ideas as to what would help. There was a part of me that was frustrated. Not with her, but with myself for not having been able to help her do the deed. But there was another part of me that wasn't completely bothered because it meant I got to have sex with her again. I'd told her during the first time that I wouldn't finish if she didn't, but I never promised I wouldn't get myself off, which was what happened every time I got home from her house. I was only human, after all. Besides, if I was always pent up before we got down to it, there was no way I'd ever be able to last as long as I did.

"Can you imagine?" She laughed at the suggestion, but I'd been serious. Okay, half serious.

"I sure can."

"Don't start when I can't do anything about it."

"We can meet up earlier if you can leave work." I waited until the engine revving in the background on her end died down before speaking again. "I was thinking you could come to my place tonight. Doing it at yours, in your space, doesn't seem to be helping, so I thought we could switch it up."

"I can't."

"Why?"

"Because I can't."

"Again... why?"

Was this going to be the conversation where she informed me about a meet up with Dr. Derek? If so, how would I react? I couldn't forbid her to see him, even though every fiber of my being told me to. But not only would that not go over well with her, possibly ending this arrangement we had, but I had no claim on her, other than her body, which was only temporary.

Her frustration came through loud and clear when she breathed heavily into the phone.

"Because I got my period this morning."

"Oh." Did I detect a wave of disappointment in her voice? "We can do other stuff."

In a hushed tone, she responded with "I'm not doing anal."

I couldn't help my bubble of laughter. "I didn't mean that." I paused for effect. "Now that you mention it, it could be the trick. Hmmmm."

"Nope. Not gonna happen."

"Ever?" I asked, curious if she was dead set against the act.

"Hold on. You said you didn't mean that. So, what were you talking about?"

Points to her for deflecting. "I meant we could hang out, have fun with our clothes on."

"Ummm... I guess." She sounded unsure, and the last thing I wanted was for her to start rattling off reasons why we shouldn't hang out unless we were having sex. I didn't want to hear about boundaries and all the crap she tried to lay on me once before.

Before she could think too much about it, I said, "I'll swing by your place later. What time are you done working?"

"I should be finished by five thirty."

"Good. I'll be over at six. Go straight home. Don't stop anywhere."

"Why?"

"Trust me."

After we hung up, I realized I only had two and a half hours to pull my plan together.

22

OLIVIA

"Ollie!"

"I'm upstairs. I'll be right down," I shouted back, pulling on my most comfortable sweatshirt and shorts. I'd had massive cramps all day, and only after having taken a hot shower and some pain reliever, had they started to wane. With my hair twisted up into a messy top knot, I glanced in the mirror one more time.

Should I let him see me like this? Would his attraction toward me disappear if he saw me dressed in unflattering clothing, no makeup, and damp hair? As I teetered between making a decision, I figured if he could think I was still sexy in my work overalls, the clothes I had on now weren't too much of a stretch to the other side.

Rounding the corner, I took a deep breath to steady the bout of nerves that overtook me when I heard his voice minutes ago. The rustling of paper bags told me I'd find Luke in the kitchen. When I entered, he looked up from the island, his hand buried inside one of the bags.

"I figured you'd be hungry, so I picked you up a few things. Comfort food." When all I could do was stare at him, surprised he'd gone to any effort for me, he frowned. "Don't women get cravings on their period?"

"I guess."

"You guess?"

"I mean, yeah, sometimes." He walked toward me with a hoagie in his hand, pecking my lips before motioning toward the stool for me to sit.

"I got you a meatball sub from Roma's, extra cheese." Luke tore open the white wrapping and I inhaled the delicious aroma. These subs were my favorite.

"I can't believe you remembered I liked these."

"Liked? You were obsessed with them. You used to eat so many I was surprised you didn't tip the scales at five hundred pounds."

"You're exaggerating," I said, my mouth watering at the sight of all the gooey, saucy goodness.

"Mark will back me up." For some reason I looked behind me, expecting to see my brother standing nearby, but it was only the two of us. "I also picked you up some broccoli cheese soup from Panera, white chocolate macadamia nut cookies from Rosalie's bakery, and good old Ben & Jerry's ice cream."

"Chocolate Cara—"

"Chocolate Caramel Cookie Dough," he finished, taking it out of the bag and putting it in the freezer.

"Why did you do all this?"

"Because I wanted to."

He leaned forward on the island, his eyes roaming over me, making me self-conscious, even though he wore a smile the entire time.

"You can barely control yourself. I know this look I've got going on is a major turn-on." I downplayed my sudden bout of insecurity by making a joke, one he didn't play into.

"You've never looked more beautiful."

"God, I hope that's not true." I shoved the end of the hoagie into my mouth before I said something embarrassing. The first bite was heaven, and when I groaned, Luke cleared his throat, pulling my attention to him and away from the meal I was trying not to devour like a wild animal.

"Is it weird I'm jealous of your hoagie?"

I nodded, swallowing another yummy bite. Afterward, I licked the side of my mouth, feeling for some sauce I knew didn't make it into my mouth.

He parted his lips to say something, but the chime of his phone had him snapping them shut. If his phone alert was anything like mine, someone was texting him. Another message came through, followed by one more.

"You can get that if you need to," I said, getting up from my seat to pour myself a drink of water.

"It's just Ben. He and some of the guys are meeting up for a few drinks."

"You can go. We can hang out another time. I have four more days of being out of commission." He rolled his eyes at my lame attempt at a joke.

"I'd rather stay here with you, if you don't mind. Besides, my knee is bothering me."

Several years ago, my dad told me about Luke's injury. Apparently, a player from the opposite team ran at him and swiped his legs out from underneath him to get the ball, and the way Luke landed took him out for the rest of the season. He tore the cartilage in his right knee and had to have two surgeries.

"Sure." Internally I did a little happy dance he wanted to stay, but at the same time I berated my bout of excitement because it could only mean one thing.

I was starting to fall for him all over again and I couldn't go down that road a second time. We could go back to being friends, but I needed to protect my heart this time around.

"Did you eat?"

"I was hoping you'd save some of your sub for me, but I guess that's not going to happen." He bore no expression and his tone was flat. I couldn't readily determine if he was messing with me. But when he extracted another sandwich from the bag, he smiled. "I knew better than to take food out of your mouth."

When I was hungry, my family would often joke I turned into a different person, and when I was in the middle of consuming some of my favorite foods, they said I would growl. But they lied. I wasn't quite that dramatic.

We sat in silence, side by side, and ate our dinners. After we'd finished, him before me even though I'd started first and was famished, I threw away the deli papers and placed my glass in the sink. When I turned around, Luke was in front of me, invading my personal space. Standing so close I could smell the sauce on his breath. Or was that mine?

"Did you need something?"

His gaze lowered to my mouth, but what he said didn't coincide with what I thought he wanted to do. "Do you want to watch a movie?"

"Did you have a particular one in mind?"

"I'll let you pick."

He reached for my hand, and I let him take it, entwining my fingers with his as he led me toward the living room. While scrolling through Prime and Netflix for something to watch, we talked about how he was adjusting to being back in Vegas after being gone so long. Afterward, he asked me about work, sharing in my irritation when I regaled a few of the stories where male customers didn't want to deal with me simply because I was a woman.

An hour later, we finally settled on a movie. Or should I say I did, because he didn't care about period piece flicks, especially foreign films set in the early 1800s. But he didn't say a word when I hit Play.

We started off sitting close on the couch, but as my dinner

slowly digested, I became tired, shifting to lie down, my legs bent so I didn't take up any of his room. But he grabbed my legs and put them over his lap. When he rubbed my feet, it was the beginning of the end of my conscious state.

His fingers were magical, as I was already all too aware.

Halfway through the movie, we'd somehow moved into a horizontal position, him spooning me from behind with his arms wrapped around me to anchor us together. Because I enjoyed this position way too much, I almost moved to sit up, but in the end decided against it.

What would be the harm in falling asleep wrapped up in Luke's warm embrace? It was only going to happen this one time.

OLIVIA

"Where are you?" Brooke asked, the rushed tone to her voice indicating she had something to tell me.

"Luke convinced me to come to one of his practices. I'm sitting in the parking lot, deciding if this is a good idea or not."

"We talked about this. You need to let all that stuff from the past go."

"I know, and I am."

Three days had passed since we fell asleep on the couch, and every day since our interactions had become much of the same. Us having dinner at my house, talking for hours, and falling asleep while watching a movie.

In the silence that followed, I contemplated leaving, but my undecisive plan was thwarted when Luke headed straight for me. He was dressed in white shorts, a blue T-shirt, and a base-ball cap turned backward. I hadn't seen him dressed like this in a long time, and while his attire was strictly for practice, there was something sexy about the way he wore it. Call me weird, but his clothes turned me on. Or maybe that was just the man in general.

"Are you still there?" More silence as I continued to devour the sight of him. "Hello?"

"Sorry. Luke just walked up. Was there a specific reason you were calling me?"

"I was going to ask you if you wanted to join me and Kate for a spa day on Friday."

"Kate?" My eyes were still on him as he stopped to talk to one of his teammates, peering over at me every few seconds. Berating myself for not focusing on what my best friend was saying, I looked away from him and at the steering wheel instead. "Who's Kate?"

"Someone I met at work." There was a hint of excitement wrapped up in her voice.

"Someone you might like?"

"Maybe." She was being coy, which wasn't like her. "We get my employee discount, so it'll be the full work up."

"How could I say no?"

"You can't. Listen, I have to go but I'll call you later and we'll talk more about it."

"Can't wait."

The second I ended the call, Luke and his teammate separated, and he waltzed over, wearing one of his panty-dropping smiles. He opened the door and extended his hand. I could get out of my vehicle by myself, but I accepted his chivalrous gesture anyway.

Before I could say a word, his lips briefly met mine, the quick greeting one would give someone they were in a relationship with, which we were not. But I didn't say anything, mainly because I liked his forwardness. These were the subtle changes that messed with my head, even though I willed them not to. But when he looked at me like he adored me, or kissed me hello as if he was my boyfriend, or even when he texted solely to say hi, my stomach would flip, and I'd wear an expression akin to true happiness.

"I'm glad you came," he said, leading me toward the field.

"Are you sure it's okay I'm here. You're not going to get in trouble?" The only other people here were the players and the coach.

"I assure you I'm not going to get in any trouble." He guided me toward the third row of the bleachers. "You'll have a good view right here. We're not doing a full practice today, so it should only be about an hour."

"Okay. I have my phone with me in case I get bored."

"Who are you kidding? You love to watch me play."

A beat passed before I said, "You might be right."

Back in the day, I used to watch him practice all the time, staying for hours on end, fascinated with how skilled he was at the game. Sometimes he knew I was there and sometimes he didn't. Those were the times when I'd lose myself to thoughts of what it would be like to be his girlfriend, to run up to him afterward and throw my arms around him and gush about how great he was, and how he was going to make it to the big league someday. But he only ever saw me as his buddy's little sister, and a friend as we got older. Nothing more.

So, it was surreal to be mixed up with him in this weird sex-deal thingy, not to mention inviting me to one of his professional practices. If I dissected it, though, I'd ruin the plethora of feelings swirling around inside me, the biggest one being joy.

Before he jogged off toward the field, he took off his cap and pushed his hair back, tossing the hat on the bench next to me.

The next hour flew by as I was mesmerized with every move he made. The ball seemed to be an extension of his foot, guarding it as if his life depended on it. He was fast, precise, and added in some fancy footwork to boot. The only way I knew he wasn't showing off because I was watching was because I'd seen him play too many times in the past, and although his technique had improved since we were kids, he played with the same level of concentration and skill.

An hour and forty-five minutes later, the practice ended. Luke caught my eye and mouthed, "Sorry," to which I waved my hand at him, letting him know it was no big deal that they were out there longer than he said they would be.

Grabbing his hat, I walked down the bleacher steps and waited by the sidelines. He was busy talking to his coach, so I pulled my phone from my back pocket and started typing out a text to Brooke. I'd gotten five words in when Ben Mathison walked up to me. I only knew who he was because he was my dad's second favorite player, Luke being the first.

Standing a couple inches shorter than Luke's six-one frame, the man was lean, with muscular thighs, as were most of these guys. His jet-black hair was cropped close to his head, and he sported a full, trimmed beard, much like what Luke had worn before he shaved. Remembering the reason why almost pulled me out of whatever interaction I was about to have with Ben. Thankfully, I hadn't lost myself too long to the memory so as not to embarrass myself by blushing.

"Who are you here with?" he asked, raising the bottom half of his shirt to wipe his face. He'd played almost as eagerly as Luke had, and I had no doubt he was hot and tired. His dark brown eyes perused my face before dipping lower, resting on my chest for several seconds before looking back up.

"I'm a friend of Luke's."

"A friend?" The way he said, "a friend?" put me on alert. I didn't know if it was his tone, or the way he tilted his head, or the way his gaze burned my skin, but I wasn't enjoying this conversation so far. Peeking around him, I noticed Luke was still engaged with his coach. Ben followed my eyeline, a smirk on his face when he turned his attention back on me. "Are you her?"

What an odd question. "Her who?"

"The chick he's helping?"

There was a moment when his question and my confusion

smashed together, and the outcome of the collision was a rush of heat through my entire body, the air in my lungs being forced out in a sputter.

"Excuse me?"

"You know. The one he's fucking. The one who can't get off."

His crassness shocked me, but it shouldn't have. I knew what he was going to say before he gave life to the words. My eyes welled up in both shock and anger. I wanted to spew something back at him, but he'd rendered me speechless.

He made things worse when he stepped into me, and because I was still in a state of shock, I didn't move back.

"If my man can't do the job, I'd like to give it a try." I flinched when he ran his finger down my arm, his touch succeeding in snapping me out of my disbelief.

Various responses begged to be thrown back at him, but I didn't utter a word as I shoved Luke's baseball cap into Ben's chest and stormed away.

My tires squealed against the asphalt of the parking lot, and from the rearview mirror, I saw Luke rushing after me, stopping only when he knew he couldn't catch me.

I rejected each of his calls as I drove home. Tears blurred my vision, and I was angry at myself for allowing him to weave his way back into my heart.

Whatever defenses I'd built up over the years should've stayed erect.

But now I was back to where I was ten years ago.

Only it was worse, because I'd been falling faster and deeper for him than I had the first time.

24

OLIVIA

IT WASN'T BAD ENOUGH MY PHONE RANG NONSTOP, BUT FIVE minutes after I'd locked myself inside my house, Luke was at my door banging. I knew it was him because he kept yelling my name, asking me why I'd run off.

The sound of my ringtone mixed with the incessant rapping on my door made me even angrier.

"Olivia, open the door. Talk to me." Moments passed and still he was relentless. "If you're not going to let me in, can you at least answer the phone?" His voice took on an edge I hadn't heard before, one of desperation. If I hadn't been as livid as I was, pacing the living room and debating on calling Mark to come over and get Luke out of here, an option I dismissed because I'd have to explain why he was here in the first place, I might have felt bad for him. Then I remembered why he sounded as desperate as he did, and my fury stomped on the ounce of pity I had for him.

This was all his fault. He had to brag about poor Olivia, the woman who couldn't come during sex. What else had he divulged to Ben? Did he tell him everything we'd done? All the positions? What I looked like naked? How much detail did he discuss with his friend? Did he tell any of his other teammates?

The more questions that formed in my infuriated brain, the more incensed I became.

Every time the door vibrated from the use of his fist, the more my heart sped up, and the more rage slithered through my veins, only to travel up my throat and rest inside my mouth, waiting to be unleashed.

After ten minutes of him trying to get me to open the door or answer my phone, I unclicked the lock with a shaky hand, and yanked it open. Luke had his hand raised in the air, dropping his arm to his side when I suddenly appeared.

"Fuck you, Luke. I never want to see you again." I wanted to ask him countless questions, but those were the words my brain formed, never making it through the filtered part before they rushed from my lips.

He wedged his foot in the door when I tried to slam it shut on him, his shoulder braced against the wood to ensure I wouldn't accomplish what I wanted.

"I don't understand. What happened? Why are you acting like this?"

With all my weight behind me, I attempted to close the door one more time, but he used his strength to shove it open, stepping inside before I could stop him.

"Get out!"

"No. Not until you tell me why you're acting like this." Cautious steps brought him closer, but I backed away. If he dared to put his hands on me, I wouldn't be held accountable for my actions. It was as if I were outside my body, watching everything unfold, helpless to predict the outcome or control any of the tornado-like emotions spiraling through me.

He said my name numerous times, pleaded with me over and over. His expression morphed from confusion to worry to fear, his movements calculated, cautious so as not to scare me away too soon. He treated me like a wounded animal about to strike out at any moment. And that was exactly how I felt.

Helpless.

Vulnerable.

Exposed.

"Goddammit, Olivia! What happened?"

Closing my eyes so I didn't have to see his face didn't work. I even tried holding my breath, figuring if I wasn't taking air into my lungs, time would slow down long enough for me to figure a way out of this situation. But that didn't work either.

My only option was to confront him. Otherwise, being the stubborn man I knew him to be, he'd stay here all night, and my emotional strength had been all but zapped.

I stood frozen in place, keeping my arms pinned to my side because I feared I'd physically lash out at him.

"Your friend Ben asked if I was the girl you were fucking. The one who can't get off."

"What?" His voice raised two octaves with the one-word question, his brows pinched together so tightly his eyes narrowed into slits.

"And he offered to take your place."

All signs of strain on his face vanished. "What exactly did he say?" I'd seen Luke angry before, but never like this. The muscles in his jaw flexed continuously as his hands curled into tight fists.

"He said, and I quote, 'If my man can't do the job, I'd like to give it a try.'"

His head dropped and he sucked in a breath, his nostrils flaring with the action. The silence stretched between us, thick and heavy, and when I didn't think I could take the lingering quiet any longer, he spoke.

"I'm so sorry. He never should have said anything to you. I'll deal with him." His last words took on a menacing tone.

"Do you know how humiliated I am? Do you tell him every-thing we do? Do you laugh at me?"

He reached for me, but I retreated. "Of course not. I only mentioned something to him one time. I swear. And I regretted it right after I said it. You have to believe me."

"No, I don't. I should've never let my guard down around you. I knew better, but you have this uncanny ability to twist me up so badly, all my reasoning goes out the window. I vowed to never allow myself to be hurt by you a second time. But I failed. It won't happen again. This thing we had going is over."

This time when he reached for me, I wasn't quick enough to move out of the way. He grabbed my arms and pulled me into him. I struggled to get away, but it was useless. His hold was desperately strong.

"When did I hurt you the first time?"

"I'm not getting into this with you. I want you to leave." His grip tightened when I tried to break free a second time.

"Please, tell me. How is it fair if I don't even know what you're talking about?" The slight grimace he wore told me he might have an inkling as to what I'd been referring to after all.

"Nothing about this is fair," I mumbled, not wanting to dive into the past now or ever. He held my gaze until I had to look away. I could feel my heart start to splinter, and I couldn't risk losing another part of myself to him. "Just go, Luke."

"Don't do this. We're good together. And I'm not talking about the sex. Although, that's a huge bonus. For me, at least." The slight lilt to his voice told me to keep my eyes cast down-ward, otherwise I'd see the curve of his lips, and it would be so much harder to stick to my guns.

I silently repeated what Ben had said. Did I believe Luke only told him once about our deal? I hated I couldn't answer either way.

"Go."

"I'm not going anywhere until you tell me what I did."

"Go," I repeated, this time louder and with more emphasis.

"No." While his voice was raised, his hold on me loosened, allowing me to sever the contact he'd made. "Tell me."

I had two choices. I could refuse to enlighten him as to how he'd hurt me in the past, or I could confront him once and for all. If I chose the latter, perhaps I could release some of the anger and hurt he'd inflicted on me. Trust me, I had enough left in reserve to fuel the decision to stay away from him going forward.

"Do you remember the night of your eighteenth birthday party? The one you threw at your house when your parents went on vacation to Florida?"

"Yes."

I held his stare, needing him to hear every word I was about to say.

"Do you remember what happened in your room? With me?" He nodded, his shoulders coming up an inch in anticipation. Or was that regret? Maybe a dash of shame? "I offered myself to you, but you rejected me. I was in love with you, and you tossed me aside like I was nothing. Did you know you were my first kiss? I thought you were special. I was ready. To be with you. I wanted you. But you didn't want me." He began to speak, but I cut him off, needing to expel everything before I lost the nerve and continued to keep it all bottled up inside. "I could have handled the rejection, in time, but you took Amanda Kneely to your bedroom. She was good enough for you to sleep with, but I wasn't. And let's not forget you ignored me for an entire week before you left. I never heard a word from you until I saw you at McConley's."

"You have no idea how much I wanted to be with you that night. To be your first. Hell, I wanted to be your last, but I'd gotten accepted to UCLA on a full soccer scholarship, and I didn't want to take your virginity and leave. And I didn't have sex with Amanda. I wanted to, but only to forget about what you offered to me." His features twisted ruefully. "That's not how it sounds. I was so messed up that night, I just wanted a distraction." He was in front of me now, caressing the side of my face. "I didn't know you loved me, Ollie."

When he said my nickname this time, my eyes welled.

"I'm so sorry. I should have told you why I turned you down, but I'd been drinking, and you surprised me with what you wanted to do. I was trying to deal with my feelings for you." He paused, giving both of us time to digest everything. "Communication isn't big on the list for teenagers, I suppose, especially guys."

"Why didn't you ever call me after you left?"

"I wanted to let some time pass before I reached out, assuming you might be upset with me for not taking you up on your offer. But days passed into weeks, and weeks into months. Before I knew it, three years had gone by and I figured my effort would be too little too late. When I saw you at the bar, though, I knew I had to say something. Never in a million years did I think we'd end up here."

Admittedly, some of my anger had subsided, but I was still hurt, and I didn't know how to process these feelings, on top of everything else he'd told me. I needed space from him. From us.

With a faux sense of strength, I stood taller. "I need you to leave."

"But I don't want to. I want to stay and work this out."

"And what *I* want is some distance from you."

"For how long?"

"I don't know."

"Olivia." His bottom lip disappeared between his teeth, his anxiousness written into every line of his face, housed in the tense muscles of his body. "Don't end this. I'm sorry for how I handled things all those years ago, and I'm sorry I mentioned our arrangement to Ben. Like I said, he's going to be dealt with."

I barely allowed five seconds to pass before I said, "You need to go now."

All he could manage to do at this point was shake his head because his words hadn't accomplished a damn thing. He slowly headed for the door a moment later. Right before he walked out, he turned back to look at me, and the downtrodden expression on his face made me want to call him back and tell him everything was okay.

But I didn't.

I couldn't.

This wasn't about Luke or how he felt.

This was about me, and how I needed time to figure out what I wanted to do next.

25

LUKE

Nursing my bruised knuckles didn't assuage the need for vindication I still harbored. I'd gone to Ben's house after leaving Olivia, but he wasn't home. I'd waited for three hours, and when there was still no sign of him, and my calls to him went unanswered, I decided to confront him at practice the next day.

Which was why my hand throbbed, and why the corner of my mouth stung whenever I ran my tongue over the cut I now sported.

He'd had one foot on the ground when I gripped him up and dragged him out of his vehicle, surprising him with a hit to his jaw. He stumbled back in shock, throwing up his hands to defend himself when I came at him again, catching him in the ribs. When the shock of my attack wore off seconds later, he rushed me and we fell to the asphalt, exchanging blows until Andy and Tom rushed over, as well as some of the other guys, to pull us off each other.

"I don't know what's going on with you two," Coach said, "but you're not going to bring that shit on the field. Go home."

I'd never been thrown out of a practice or a game before. An argument rested on my lips, but Coach was right. I couldn't

SIMPLY COMPLICATED | 165

speak for Ben, but if I stayed, I wouldn't do anything but be a burden on the team. My attitude sucked right now, and I'd only be distracted on the field.

I sped out of the lot and contemplated showing up at the garage, but figured an unannounced visit wouldn't work in my favor, so I drove home.

An hour later, I was halfway to drunk and no closer to knowing how to handle things with Olivia going forward.

26

OLIVIA

"THANKS AGAIN. YOU HAVE NO IDEA HOW MUCH I NEED THIS. Anything to take my mind off *him* is welcome."

Two days had passed since my blowout with Luke. He'd texted me a total of four times after he left my house to tell me how sorry he was. But since then... nothing. I was both relieved and disappointed, the combination confusing me even more than I was already.

The first call I placed after he'd left was to Brooke, of course. She offered to come over, but I told her I wanted to be alone. I just wanted to talk through a few things. Her unwavering support was a huge comfort, and even though she told me not to make any rash decisions while I was still in the thick of all my anger and hurt, she also told me to make him sweat it out a bit. He deserved it for opening his mouth to his friend. Yes, Brooke knew about the happenings between me and Luke, but she was there for the first encounter when he offered to help me out. Some details I kept to myself, but some I chose to share with her. She was my best friend, my anchor when I needed to be grounded, talked off the ledge, and given a pep talk.

"A good pedicure will take your mind off almost anything."

I sighed in agreement when the woman working on me kneaded some of the tension from my foot. In my relaxed state I'd almost forgotten someone else was here with us. Kate, the woman Brooke was interested in, someone who also worked here at the casino with her, sat on the other side of my friend. Her eyes were closed, and a satisfied smile rested on her lips. She appeared to be enjoying the services as well.

Her poker straight, dark blonde hair hit right above her shoulders, her almond-shaped eyes a beautiful shade of amber. I could see why Brooke liked her, not to mention she had a figure I'd kill for. For all her attributes, she wasn't the typical woman Brooke went after. Kate seemed almost innocent. No tattoos. No piercings. Nothing that screamed bad girl, appearance wise, at least. My bestie had several tattoos and was working on another. As for piercings, she had both of her nipples done.

"Kate, how are you liking Vegas?" I asked, startling her relaxed state. She glanced at Brooke before answering.

"It's different from Mississippi where I grew up, but that's what I like about it." Her eyes veered to mine briefly before looking back at the woman next to her.

"Give it time and you'll never want to live anywhere else." Brooke's voice took on a seductive edge, and for a moment I felt like I was intruding on a private moment shared between them. Not that I wasn't used to Brooke hitting on someone, but there was something different about the way she looked at Kate. Watching their interaction only made me miss Luke, a sentiment I shoved back down because there was no way I was willing to acknowledge that fact.

For the next three hours, we pampered ourselves with additional services. The sauna and the massage were my favorite, the pedicure a close third. As we were about to part ways, Brooke pulled me aside, out of earshot of Kate.

"What do you think?"

"Of what?" She could've been referring to a number of topics, and before I blurted anything out, I wanted to be sure.

"Of Kate."

I smiled at the tiny bit of trepidation in her voice. She liked this one. A lot. More than anyone before her.

"She's really nice."

"Almost too nice."

"Oh Lord." I sighed. "Don't mess this up because she doesn't come with drama. That's never gone well for you in the past."

"I know." She waved her hand in the air, and when I thought she was going to say something else about Kate, she mentioned Luke.

"Are you going to keep sleeping with him?"

"I don't know. I want to, but I think if we keep this up, we're only prolonging the inevitable."

"Which is what?"

"I don't know," I repeated, my thoughts too twisted around the other to make sense of them.

"I say you keep going. You still haven't screamed out his name yet."

Her shoulder bumped mine and the wiggle of her brows made me chuckle. I wanted to tell her I had in fact yelled his name, but just not as a result of an orgasm.

Will it ever happen? Do I want to keep going to find out? Can I move on from our argument and trust he won't embarrass me again?

"I'm afraid—"

"We've already gone over this, Liv. Don't punish him for the past, for a mistake or miscommunication or whatever you want to call it when he was eighteen. Would you want to be judged on shit you did when you were a teenager? I know I wouldn't want to be. I don't want to be judged on stuff I did last month." She slung her arm over my shoulder. "And he's apologized for what happened with his buddy." She took a quick breath. "Listen, if he does anything again to piss you off this badly, I'll take care of him for you."

"Meaning?"

"I can think of some creative ways to get back at him."

I didn't ask for details because I didn't really want to know. All I cared about was that Brooke had my back, no matter what.

The entire drive home, I teetered between calling Luke, and letting things fizzle out. But the thought of not seeing him anymore twisted me up more than the memory of being embarrassed by Ben. And after taking the time to allow Luke's apology to sink in, I believed he was sorry for the role he played in what happened the other day, and in the past.

Plus, I'd agreed to be his date to his sister's wedding, which was coming up soon. And he'd kept his end of the bargain, trying his hardest to help me orgasm. It wouldn't be right for me to end things just yet.

LUKE

I'D BEEN RESTING ON THE COUCH WHEN MY CELL ALERTED ME TO a text. Removing the ice pack from my knee, I walked the few paces to unhook it from the charger. When Olivia's name flashed on the screen, I was both excited and fearful to see what her message said. Feeling unsure of where I stood in her life was torture. I wanted more from her but couldn't ask for it. Not now. Not after Ben basically ruined things for me.

We had practice together every day, but I still haven't said another word to him. In time, I was sure I'd forgive him. He was one of my best friends, but what he said to her was inexcusable. Not so much letting her know he was aware of what was going on between me and her, but offering to step in and have sex with her. He'd crossed so many lines, I couldn't even count them.

In all honesty, he'd been on edge and a bit of a prick ever since his ex, Vicky, dumped his ass. But even that didn't excuse his behavior.

When I finally mustered up the balls, I swiped the screen and read her message.

Can you come over?

She could be asking me to stop by to end things officially, after having thought more about it, or she could want to continue with what we'd been doing.

As I expelled my breath, my fingers selected the necessary letters for my response.

Be there in a half hour

The sun had set by the time I arrived on her doorstep. I didn't knock right away, needing extra time to prepare in case she was going to, in fact, end things between us. What could I say to convince her otherwise if that was the case? Profess my feelings for her? Tell her she'd been the one I'd always dreamed about being with? Beg her to be with me? I could remind her that she promised to go to my sister's wedding as my date. There was a good chance guilt could work if everything else failed.

None of those scenarios seemed appealing, but I'd do whatever I'd have to in order to get her to change her mind if she were going to take a step back.

Before my knuckles connected with the wood, the door swung open. Olivia stood before me in a red lace teddy. It must've been among the items I'd bought her at La Perla. The saleswoman chose well when she included this piece.

"Come in."

She moved aside so I could enter, but I didn't get far before she gently grabbed my chin and moved my head to the side. "What happened to your lip?" Before she allowed me time to answer, her focus swung to my reddened knuckles.

"I told you I'd deal with Ben. And I did."

"Are you okay?"

Her concern touched me, but for as much as Ben and I went at each other, we were both fine.

"I'm good."

Taking in the sight of her, all thoughts of my altercation perished. The urge to rip the sheer material from her body and take her right there in the entryway to her house was strong. But I didn't make a move as I stood a foot away from her, working to control the baser need flaring to life inside me.

Finally, after what seemed like forever, I stepped closer and placed my hands on her waist. "You being dressed like this... does it mean what I think it does?"

"And what would my nightgown have to do with anything?" A ghost of a smile passed over her lips.

"You're not wearing a nightgown."

She looked down at herself. "What is it?"

"It's something you wear when you want to get fucked."

"Is that so?"

The pinch of her brows made me think I'd misread what I thought was a signal from her. But when her teeth toyed with her bottom lip, I knew she was playing with me.

I moved to pull her closer, but she put her hands on my chest to keep the distance.

"What's wrong?"

"I didn't ask you to come over so we could have sex."

"Oh. Do you still have your period?"

"No."

My frown matched hers from seconds before. "Why are you dressed like that?" Her hardened nipples strained against the lace, making my mouth water with the need to wrap my lips around them.

"Because I needed something to wear to bed and I thought this one was pretty." *Is she messing with me?*

"So why am I here?"

"I wanted to tell you I'm not going to stop doing this." She gestured between us. "After thinking about it, I believe you never intentionally set out to hurt me ten years ago or the other day, even though that was exactly what happened." I sucked in a breath to interrupt, to apologize once more, but she placed her hand over my mouth. "I know you're sorry. You don't have to tell me again." She replaced her hand with her lips, but when I tried to deepen the kiss, she pulled back. "We're not doing anything tonight. You're going to leave and think about me in this outfit."

"Seriously?"

"Yup. This is your punishment."

"And there's nothing I can do to change your mind?" She smacked my hands away when I tried to pull her into me.

"No."

"This sucks. But I'd rather go home and have a major case of blue balls than be heartbroken because you broke things off." I hadn't meant to show my cards, but there was no point in disguising how I felt about her. Not anymore.

She didn't comment on the latter part of my statement, instead focusing on what I'd said first.

"Don't you constantly have a state of blue balls when you're with me? You don't ever finish."

"I do when I go home."

"Good for you."

The smirk on her face told me she wasn't upset by this news. I never promised not to come at all, just not while we were having sex.

We stared at each other for the next couple minutes, which seemed like an eternity because neither one of us said a word. If any more time passed in silence, I was going to throw her over my shoulder and work on convincing her to change her mind as I hurried toward her bedroom.

Oddly, I was the one who chose to speak first. "Did you want to get together tomorrow?"

"I can't."

"Why?"

"I have plans."

"You and Brooke doing something? Or are you having dinner at your parents' house?" I paused a beat before asking, "Is your mom still trying to set you up?" The thought alone made me upset.

"No." She shifted from one foot to the other, lowering her eyes from mine.

"No?"

"No to all three questions."

"Then why can't I come over tomorrow?"

"Because I... I'm... I'm going on a date."

"A date," I muttered. "Who with?" The tone I used was calm, but I was a mess on the inside.

"Derek."

"The doctor?" That time my voice wasn't as serene, the harshness to my question causing her to raise her eyes to me once more. My heart fell into my stomach, and all I wanted to do was rant and rave, but acting in such a way wouldn't do me any good. In fact, she'd probably kick me out and ban me from coming here ever again. I had to play this smart. "Where are you going?"

"Nice try. I'm not telling you. You'll just show up and intimidate him."

"He's that much of a wuss?"

"He's not a wuss at all." I didn't appreciate her defending him. Not one bit.

"Fine. But I want you to stop by my place afterward. I'll text you the address."

"I can meet you back here."

"No. It's time you come over. Besides, I have something special planned for you."

"Care to tell me what it is?"

"Not a chance." She ushered me toward the front door. *I*

guess I'm leaving now. Before she kicked me out, I leaned in until my mouth hovered over hers. "Remember to keep the date PG."

"You don't have to remind me. I know the rules. No sex."

"Good." I pulled back without kissing her and she pouted. *That'll teach her for toying with me.*

28

OLIVIA

Rooting through my closet to see what options I had for my date with Derek, I found a periwinkle-colored dress I'd bought two years ago on a whim but never wore. It was strapless with a fitted bodice. But the skirt flared out and away from my body. The dress even had pockets, which I thought was a sensible feature. Tossing it on the bed, I reentered my closet and found the perfect pair of nude heels to go with it.

"Are you sure you want to do this?" Brooke asked, leaning against my headboard, mindlessly scrolling through Instagram.

"Why wouldn't I?"

"Because you're already involved with Luke."

"But we're not dating." Cinching my robe tighter, I opened and closed my dresser drawers, pulling out a few options for underwear before deciding on a white satin thong.

"Did you tell Derek about Luke?"

"That we're having sex to see if he can help me come during the act?" I laughed because her question was ridiculous. "Of course, I didn't tell him. Why would I? I'm only going out on one date with the guy."

"What if you decide you like him and go out on another date?"

"So what?" I wasn't sure where this conversation was headed, but my gut told me Brooke would keep at it unless I shut her down. "Look. It's only dinner. I'm not going to sleep with him. Luke knows. I told him yesterday."

"What did he say?"

"What could he say? He can't tell me I can't go."

"He's a better man than me."

"Did you just refer to yourself as a man?"

She tossed a pillow at me. "You know what I mean." I threw the pillow back at her. "How would you feel if Luke told you he had a date."

"I'd be fine with it as long as he promised not to sleep with her." Was I lying? I didn't want to think so, but the flip of my stomach indicated I might be fooling myself.

"You keep telling yourself that."

"Do you think I can get away with wearing no bra?" I asked, pointing toward the dress. I needed a subject change. The last thing I wanted to think about was Luke, and the question she posed about if the roles were reversed.

Brooke leaned forward and inspected the garment. "You should be good. It looks like there's built-in pads." I walked into the bathroom, but apparently she wasn't done grilling me. "What else did Luke say about tonight?"

"He wants me to come by his place afterward. I told him I would." I didn't tell her that he also said he had a surprise for me. Talk of the man needed to end and now.

"Be careful, Liv. I'd hate for you to ruin something before it even had a chance to develop." I didn't need to ask who she referred to because she was team Luke all the way.

After I finished my hair and makeup, I pulled the dress over my head and smoothed down the skirt. I turned around and inched closer to her, moving my hair to one side so she could zip me up. The final step was to slide my feet into the heels. It took me a moment to get used to the feel of them because I hadn't worn anything other than sneakers and ballet flats in what felt like forever.

"How do I look?" I did a little twirl for Brooke, hoping for an extra boost of confidence because I was suddenly in short supply.

"Fantastic."

Checking the time, I deemed I was going to be late if I didn't get a move on. I'd agreed to meet Derek at Luciano's, an upscale Italian restaurant located just off the strip. Without any traffic issues, it would take me twenty minutes to get there, which was only five more than I had right now.

"I have to go."

Brooke didn't say a word as she followed me outside, standing behind me while I locked the front door. When I turned to face her, she looked something akin to disappointed, but perhaps I misread her expression. She wasn't on board with me going out on a date with someone who wasn't Luke, but I wasn't going to allow her hesitations to become mine. I'd dealt with enough emotional ups and downs over the past few days to last me for quite some time to come.

After promising I'd call her tomorrow, I folded myself behind the wheel of my Jeep and left for my date. Luckily, I arrived with two minutes to spare. Derek stood near the entrance, and the nervousness I'd attempted to push way deep down resurfaced. His dark blue suit accentuated his broad shoulders, the first button of his crisp white shirt undone, making me a touch more comfortable. For some reason, the lack of a tie put me at ease, even though both of us were dressed up. His wavy hair was perfectly styled, the richness of the dark-colored tresses a perfect contrast to his green eyes. There was no doubt this man turned many a head, and although he didn't cause a flutter in my belly like a certain soccer player, I was looking forward to getting to know him better.

"Wow. You look amazing." He reached for my hand and pulled me closer, placing a kiss on my cheek.

"Thank you. So do you."

"It's been a minute since I've worn a suit. I'm happy it still fits." When he ushered me inside and toward the hostess, I released any guilt and apprehension I'd felt on the ride here.

I never admitted this to Brooke, but in a small way I felt like I was cheating on Luke, even though he knew about my date. Of course, I wasn't going to sleep with the guy, but there was a possibility he was going to kiss me afterward. Would I let him? Luke and I said no sex with anyone else, but we never said anything about a kiss. The bout of apprehension I'd just released came back full force with the bombardment of thoughts. Luckily, Derek wasn't any the wiser to my internal dilemma.

Once we were seated and had placed our drink orders, I opened the menu. There were eight pages of options, and as I lost myself to scouring the choices, he cleared his throat.

When I looked over at him, the dimple in his right cheek made an appearance.

"If you're not sure what to order, I can make a recommendation. I've been here before."

"Sure. I'm not a picky eater."

"Are you allergic to seafood?"

"No."

He closed his menu, and gently removed mine from my hands, placing both toward the edge of the table. A quick jerk of his chin toward the waiter and our server was next to us.

"We're both going to have the risotto with shrimp." As soon as Derek uttered the word risotto, Luke's face popped into my head. The dish, minus the shrimp, was one of his favorites. As if he sensed he'd entered my mind, a text came through. I didn't have to check to see it was him. Every fiber in my being told me it was. A second alert sounded, followed by a third. "You can check that if you want. I won't think you're being rude. Trust me, I'm sure my pager will go off at some point."

"I didn't know they still used pagers."

"Hospitals are notorious for being dead zones for cell service, but that's on purpose. Many of the walls were built to keep X-rays from going through, which makes it nearly impossible for cell phone signals to penetrate as well. But there's something about the signal the pagers use that doesn't have any issues. It's why we still use them."

"I didn't know all that."

"Neither did I up until a couple years ago when I thought to ask." The curve of his mouth should have tempted me to have thoughts about pressing my lips to his, but the only person I could think about kissing was the man who sent me yet another text message.

"Sorry. Let me turn my phone off."

"Seems like someone wants to get a hold of you," he said, his left brow arching slightly.

"Probably my mom," I lied. "But I'll call her back later." I did happen to glance at the screen as I powered down the device, and as I suspected, Luke's name appeared as the sender of the texts.

"Tell me, Olivia. How is it you're single?"

"I could ask you the same thing. You're more of a catch."

"How so?"

"Being a doctor for one. Plus, you're young and handsome. And minus the misunderstanding when I first met you, you seem to be a nice guy."

"I may say stupid stuff sometimes, but I do think I'm a nice guy. I'll agree with you." His dimple showed up again. "Being a doctor has its drawbacks, though, mainly the long hours. But I have to pay my dues." He took a sip of his wine. "And you're wrong."

"About what?"

"You're the better catch. Not only are you gorgeous, but any woman who works on cars is a bonus in my book. Like I said before, I can barely change my oil. In fact, I only attempted it once and it didn't go well."

Over the course of the next hour and a half, we talked about various subjects, from our jobs to which movies we'd seen recently to what we liked to do in our spare time. He liked to be outdoors whenever he encountered the opportunity, hiking and fishing being the main two activities he enjoyed. I told him I wasn't much of an outdoor person, but I wasn't opposed to trying new things, which after I thought about it, sounded more like an invitation for him to invite me to do something. On paper, this guy was a dream. And while I thought he was attractive, smart, and charming, he didn't hold a candle to Luke. I didn't regret coming here tonight, but I wouldn't be agreeing to another date if he asked. It wouldn't be fair to lead him on knowing my heart belonged to someone else.

I wanted to be shocked at my thought, but it was pointless to pretend I wasn't head over heels for Luke. That didn't mean I would make my feelings known to him. I couldn't allow him to have the upper hand again. My heart couldn't take another devastation.

"I had a great time." Derek's hand rested on the small of my back as he walked me to my Jeep. "I'd love to do this again sometime."

I should tell him the truth, or part of the truth, at least. That I had a good time, as well, but this would be as far as it went. But I chickened out.

"Me too" was my response, pulling my keys from my purse.

When I'd unlocked my door, he reached for the handle and opened it for me. I parted my lips to thank him, but he leaned in close before I could say anything. With a soft press of his mouth to mine, he kissed me, lingering for a few seconds before pulling back. If my head hadn't been so wrapped around another man, I would've appreciated the feel of his mouth on mine, but somehow the action felt more like a betrayal on my part.

"Have a good night, Olivia."

He stepped back and allowed me to situate myself in the driver seat. Afterward, he closed the door, smiling at me as I turned over the engine.

As I pulled away, I mindlessly touched my lips. The action wasn't because Derek had kissed me. It was because I feared Luke would ask if he did.

29

LUKE

ALL MY TEXTS HAD GONE UNANSWERED, BUT DID I REALLY EXPECT
her to respond while she was on a date?

I must've looked at my watch a thousand times, becoming
more irritated the longer I didn't hear from her. Was she going
to change her mind and not come over? Was her date going so
well they decided to do something else afterward? The thought
alone infuriated me, and I realized, as if I didn't know it already,
that Olivia wasn't leaving my house until she agreed to be
with me.

No more just friends who were sleeping together to accomplish a goal.

No more of her being set up and going on dates with
random guys.

After she stopped talking to me for two days because of
what happened with Ben, I was lucky she wanted to continue
our arrangement, and I was willing to let it be just that. But
when she told me about this date, possessiveness speared
through me, and I wanted to forbid her from going. Exerting
any kind of control over her life, however, wouldn't end well for
me, so I kept my mouth shut.

Pacing near the front door did nothing but keep me amped up, but when headlights approached, I released one breath after another with the hope I'd be able to calm myself enough that she didn't know how worked up I was. Stewing in uncertainty and jealousy wasn't a good combination, the increased thrum of my heart a perfect indicator.

I flung open the door as Olivia walked up the front steps, her eyes widening at the sudden surprise of me standing before her.

"I think this place is too small for you." Her teasing tone worked to ease a quarter of the anxiety still rushing through me.

"I thought so too, but it'll have to do." I grabbed her hand and pulled her inside, and for once she didn't try to sever the contact.

"I need a tour. Like right now."

"No way. I'll give you one later. I've waited all day for this."

She started to speak but abruptly stopped when I dragged her toward the stairs. Once we were in my bedroom, I backed her against the wall, towering over her. I hooked a finger under her chin and raised her head until her eyes met mine.

"Did you wear that dress for him or for me?"

My intention was to ask the question in a calm tone, but I couldn't hide the growl in my voice. As my eyes scoured the length of her, jealousy dominated all other emotions. Not only was her dress strapless, but it barely hit her midthigh. Her hair fell down her back, and the image of twisting the strands between my fingers and pulling while I took her from behind barreled into my brain. She looked amazing, and I hated another man had her attention for the past couple hours. Staring at her and probably imagining taking her in various positions, filling each one of her holes more than once. The mental torture I put myself through was enough to drive me insane, but because Olivia had no idea what thoughts ran through my head, she stood there innocently staring at me. And perhaps she *was* innocent, but that didn't stop the fire from burning inside me, tempting me to combust where I stood.

"I wanted to look presentable."

"Are you going to see him again?" My thumb caressed along her jaw, my fingers gripping the back of her head so she couldn't move.

"No." Her quick answer was exactly the one I hoped for.

"Did you kiss him?"

Even though my hold prevented her from moving, she cast her eyes downward, the simple gesture telling me what I didn't want to know. I should've never asked, but I did, and now I had to deal with the consequences.

I stewed in the silence that followed, and when I thought she was going to make me repeat my question, she sputtered out a breath, the word falling from her lips in a nervous whisper.

"Yes."

"Show me."

"What?" The frown marring her face matched the confusion churning inside me at having spoken those two syllables.

"Show me how you kissed him."

"*He* kissed me," she clarified. I didn't want to get into semantics with her, but regardless of who kissed who, her lips were on another man. Did it make me feel any better that she hadn't initiated the action? I wasn't sure yet because all I kept picturing was her swept up in a moment that should've never happened.

"Show me."

"No."

"Do it."

Although I tried to prevent it, anger colored my voice. She attempted to take a step back, but I clutched her waist and barred the movement.

When she realized there was no getting out of this, she leaned up on her tiptoes, parted her lips slightly and covered my mouth with hers, holding for a count of three seconds, which was two and a half seconds too long.

"Did he use his tongue? And don't lie to me."

"No, he didn't."

"Did you want him to?" *Why am I torturing myself?*

"No. I didn't even know he was going to kiss me until he did. I suspected he might, but…"

"But what?"

"I wasn't prepared. Not completely."

"Did you like kissing another man while I'm sitting here waiting for you?" *Seriously… stop.*

"Of course, I didn't," she said. "I don't want to admit this, to you or myself, but I felt like I was betraying you, even though I didn't do anything wrong."

With her admission, I squashed some of my jealousy. She could pretend all day she didn't feel something for me, other than sexual attraction, but her façade had just been obliterated.

Pushing her dress up, my fingers skimmed over the edge of her panties. "Your mouth is mine. You're not allowed to kiss anyone else but me."

I bunched the soft material in my hand and pulled, shredding the fabric in one motion. Her lips parted on a gasp, and I couldn't restrain myself any longer. Tossing the torn panties to the side, I spun her around, unzipped her dress and yanked it down until the garment pooled at her feet. She was completely naked, and it took everything in me not to kick her legs apart, bend her over, and fuck her senseless.

I hadn't lied when I told her I had a surprise for her tonight, but if I surrendered to the need to lose myself inside her, I would be no closer to making her come than I had been any other time we'd had sex.

Moving her hair to rest over her shoulder, I leaned in, my mouth close to her ear. "I have another deal for you," I said, circling my arm around her waist and pulling her into me, her ass pressing against my excitement. "If I make you come tonight, you'll agree to be mine. No more of us just having sex. I want you. All of you."

"Are you sure that's a deal you want to make?" A blend of curiosity and hope filled her voice, and because she hadn't immediately shut me down, I harnessed the encouragement I needed to keep going.

But I needed to look into her eyes when I spoke this next part. Spinning her around, I seized both of her wrists and raised her arms above her head, holding them in place with one of mine. Licking at the seam of her lips, she didn't wait long until she opened her mouth for me.

But I didn't kiss her.

Not yet.

"Absolutely. And I'm confident what I have planned for you will be exactly what you need. You might even come more than once."

"You're confident."

"I am." My fingers glided over her breast, pinching her nipple with more pressure than I'd ever used before. "Do you trust me?"

"I do," she uttered, her breath rushing forth when my fingers dipped between her thighs.

"Good. From this point on, you'll do as I say, no questions asked. Understand?"

She lowered her head before raising it again, but her silent agreement wasn't good enough for me. I needed her verbal answer. I lingered in the silence, confident I wouldn't need to ask her again. Seconds later, she spoke.

"Yes. I understand."

"Tonight will still be about you, but I'm going to be selfish, do things to you for my own enjoyment." I didn't ask if she was okay with my statement because she'd already given her consent. "You're drenched." I spread her excitement up to her clit, pinching her much like I'd done to her nipple, only slightly gentler. "You're looking forward to what I might do to you, aren't you?"

This time I accepted her nod, removing my fingers from her warmth and kissing her with such intensity I almost forgot I needed to go slow.

Be precise.

Tease her until she begged me to fuck her.

"What if you do something I don't like?" She'd been quiet for so long I wondered if she was ever going to ask me something.

"Tell me to stop. That simple. I'm going to test your limits, but I'll be aware of your body's reaction the entire time. But like I said, in case I do something you're not comfortable with just say 'stop'. Okay?"

"Okay." She nibbled on her bottom lip in nervousness, but from the quick expanse of her chest, she was also excited. As was I.

"Turn around." She did so without hesitation. "Keep your hands at your sides. Don't move."

I disappeared into my closet and came out with a white bag, dumping the contents onto the king-size bed.

"What are you do—"

"If you speak again without permission, I'm going to punish you."

"What does that mean?"

Was it wrong I loved that she wasn't complying?

Leaving the items scattered on the bed, I approached her from behind, running my palm over her plump ass. "I told you not to speak. Put your hands on the wall. Spread your legs." The first connection of my hand against her ass cheek pushed her forward, the second had her arching her back, and the third hit forced a moan from her, the sound telling me what I already knew. "I can smell your excitement," I whispered in her ear. "I knew you'd enjoy being spanked. Do you want me to redden your ass some more?" She didn't say anything, and I wondered if she was afraid to or if she was waiting for permission. "You can answer me."

"More."

This is going to be fun.

OLIVIA

"Red is a good color on you," Luke said, the sting of his palm against my backside lighting the fuse that would undoubtedly engulf me. He'd smacked my ass before, but nothing like this. His entire demeanor had switched when I walked into his house earlier. He was stern and unapologetic. I'd never seen this side of him before. At first, I thought his irritation at me having gone on a date with another man had been the root cause, and maybe it was, but he took whatever he'd been feeling and harnessed it into something else. Something sexually aggressive. Domineering.

After he spanked me three more times, the bite of pain settling into my skin and making me even more excited about what was to come, he ran his fingers through my heat, and pushed them inside me. He said I wasn't allowed to speak, and I didn't. But he didn't say anything about making noises. Grunts and moans were in abundance, forced from my throat with every touch.

With his mouth at my ear, he whispered all sorts of dirty things about what he wanted to do to me. Some of them we'd never tried before, and I could admit I was a little leery about, but he said he wouldn't push me too far, and I believed him.

His body had been pressed against me, but suddenly he was gone. I didn't turn around or ask what he was doing for fear of more punishment. Which was a conundrum because I wanted more of his brand of torment.

I was aware Luke was still in the room, somewhere behind me, but he wasn't making any noise. If he wanted me in a heightened state of awareness, he'd accomplished his goal. My entire body was alight with desire, every hair standing with anticipation, my skin covered in goose bumps.

When I didn't think I could take the silence one more second, he was back, sliding something silky over my eyes. My entire world went pitch black.

"This is so you can't see what's coming." My muscles constricted, not quite sure how to process his words. "Relax. You'll love it." He told me earlier he'd read my body's reactions, and he made good on his declaration just now. He knew I was apprehensive, so he reassured me.

He slid his palm into mine and pulled me away from the wall. I couldn't explain it, but even though I couldn't see, I was more aware of what was going on than if I'd had my sight.

After several steps, he stopped and placed my hand on the edge of the bed, moving to stand behind me.

"Crawl on top and stay on your hands and knees."

I did as he instructed, waiting for his next move. My ears pricked at the sound of him shedding his clothing, the clank of his belt buckle hitting the floor. Three beats passed before a plastic bag rustled on the bed near me.

Luke took his position behind me once more, running his hand down the middle of my backside before leaning over me and moving my hair away from my face.

"Open your mouth." I parted my lips. "Wider. Stick out your tongue." An object touched the tip of my tongue. It was hard and smooth. "Suck on it," he demanded, forcing the small item into my mouth. I swirled my tongue around the odd shape of it before he removed it, only to trail it over where his fingers had just been, pressing it against the ring of my virgin muscle.

"Luke," I whispered, anxious for what came next.

"I'll let my name slide because I know you're apprehensive." The tip of what I now believed was a butt plug breached my opening, the feeling uncomfortable. When he pushed the object in farther, a slight burning sensation followed. I couldn't stop from tensing, earning me a fierce swat to my right ass cheek. "You're not trusting me."

"I am."

He smacked me again, and I moaned. "Don't talk back." Demand and authority curled around his words, and I'd never been so turned on in my life. After another hit, and another elicit sound tearing from my throat, my muscles worked to accept the full girth of the plug. He kneaded the cheek he'd smacked, and nipped me, running his tongue over the affected area to soothe the bite of pain. "Get on your back and spread your legs."

When I moved into position, he grabbed my left ankle and wrapped something around it. A restraint, the material soft yet strong. After he'd secured my leg, he moved on to my right one. A moment later, the heat of his body enveloped me before he moved my arms to the side, one by one, working to secure them as well. In uncertainty, I struggled, and all that earned me was a harsh pinch of my nipple.

I moaned, loving the sensation shooting straight to my core. But I was a mess of conflicting emotions.

Anxious but curious.

Fearful but trusting.

Once he'd finished tying my other wrist, I tugged on all restraints, and sure enough, there was no way I was getting out of this until he released me. Being at his complete mercy was exhilarating.

"You're so turned on, you're dripping onto the sheets." His fingers slipped through my folds with ease, and when he pinched my clit, I bucked my hips. I was so sensitive, more than I'd ever been before. "Do you remember when I told you I was going to be selfish? Do things to you for my enjoyment?" I nodded. "You can speak."

"Yes."

"That's going to happen now."

The bed dipped from his weight as he straddled my waist. Seconds later his knees were on the sides of my breasts.

"What are you—"

"Enough talking. Open your mouth." His fingers were in my hair, pulling. "More."

I waited, stewing in the silence surrounding me. My breaths quickened, the anticipation causing me to squirm beneath him. The small movement made me gasp, the fullness of the plug he'd inserted reminding me I was his to do with whatever he wanted.

When I thought I couldn't take any more suspense, he slid against my tongue. I tasted the saltiness of his excitement, and I wanted more. And when I lifted my head and wrapped my lips around the tip of him, he groaned, the sound encouraging me to take him farther into my mouth. His hand was still wrapped up in my hair, and when I swirled my tongue around, he pulled tighter.

"Do it slow. Don't be greedy. Remember I can't come until you do."

Not being able to see his reaction was torture, but I complied. I teased him, nice and slow, pulling him into my mouth as far as I could manage. When he slid almost all the way out, I gently grazed my teeth over his crown. A string of expletives fell from his lips.

Only minutes after I started, he withdrew completely and moved off the bed. As if sensing my bout of insecurity, he said, "If we kept going, I was going to shoot down the back of your throat."

"Ohhhh…." My acknowledgment of what he'd said morphed into a guttural groan.

"You've used a vibrator before, right?"

"Why?"

"Answer the question."

"Yes."

A faint buzzing sound cut through the sexually charged air, and as I opened my mouth to either protest or plead, I wasn't sure which yet, he placed the device against my inner thigh, the sensation rippling through me. He teased me, running the vibrator up and down the inside of each leg, over my hip bone, even my nipples. Everywhere but where I wanted him to. No amount of begging would hasten his torment, so I remained silent.

"I wish you could see yourself. Tied to my bed, spread wide for me to do whatever I want. I could get used to this."

"Me too."

"Do you want me to fuck you with this?" The richness of his voice made me writhe almost as badly as the device in his hand. "Or do you want me to use my tongue? Or both?"

"Both."

I wanted everything he could give me. If there was a way for him to use his mouth, the device, and his cock at the same time, I would've opted for all three. But because that was impossible, I'd settle for what he offered.

The bed dipped once more when he nestled between my legs, the contrast of his warm breath and my arousal sending a chill through me. With the first swipe of his tongue, I groaned, but when he placed the vibrator against my clit, I struggled against my restraints. I was so sensitive; I didn't think I could handle the sensation.

"Stop moving."

Every time he gave me a demand, his voice took on an edge of authority, the rasp of his tone carnal, serving to spike my heart rate a little more. This Luke was different from the one I'd had sex with before. That guy was a dirty talker, eager to please, passionate, and fun. This guy was calm, focused, and domineering. I loved both versions of him, but the one who greeted me at the door when I'd arrived turned me on the most.

He tugged on the object he'd inserted at the same time he wrapped his lips around the most sensitive part of me. Again, I tried to move away from him, but couldn't because I was securely bound. His tongue flicked against me, over and over, and a familiar tingle ricocheted through me.

"Please," I cried out, not entirely sure what I was asking for. But he knew because he worked his tongue faster, before pressing the small apparatus against my clit a second time. He'd reduced the speed and the pulsations were the perfect mix of pleasure and torment.

"I want to fuck you so bad."

"Do it."

I wasn't sure how I'd feel with both him and the plug inside me, but my eagerness trumped any hesitation. And would he keep the vibrator on me as well? My breath froze in my lungs at the thought that maybe he was right. Tonight might be the night he made me come. Then I'd adhere to the deal, and I'd be his. What I didn't tell him was that when he made that deal, I'd already agreed to be his, orgasm or not. I just hadn't told him yet.

"Soon."

For the next ten minutes he worked me over. Whenever I struggled, a growl crept up his throat. When I arched my back, he'd pinch my nipple, and when I cried out it was too much, he pushed me further. We agreed I'd tell him to stop if I didn't want to continue, but the word never fell from my lips.

Being blindfolded and tied up desecrated whatever insecurities or inhibitions I'd held close in the past. It wasn't until tonight that I realized I'd never been this free before. Which seemed to be a contradiction seeing as how I wasn't free to do anything right now. Not to see. Not to wrap my arms or legs around him. Not to move, switch positions. Nothing.

I'd never felt more alive.

The tingling intensified. My breathing turned choppy, and my muscles tensed as warmth spread through me. The only other time I'd ever felt like this was right before I orgasmed. The wave was cresting. Closer. Taking on a surge more powerful than I could've imagined. I danced on the edge and was barely able to breathe, let alone tell Luke that it was going to happen.

But then he stopped. No more vibrations. No more tongue. No more fingers. In fact, he'd gotten off the bed completely.

He lifted my head to untie the blindfold, and when my eyes connected with his, he wore the smuggest grin, his left brow arched to exemplify his expression.

I'd finally found my words, forcing them from the deepest part of me. "I was so close." I failed to hide the disappointment laden around each syllable.

"I know."

"Why did you stop?"

"Because I want to see your eyes. I want to watch you unravel while I'm deep inside you. I want your focus on me while you spiral out of control."

"But what if I can't get it back?" I loved everything he'd said, but the chances I could recapture the whisper of my impending orgasm were nearly impossible. It'd taken this long to get this far, and now I feared it was all gone.

SIMPLY COMPLICATED | 197

"You can get it back because now I know what will get you off."

"And what's that?" I asked, curious as to what he thought my problem had been my entire adult life. I needed to be enlightened. *Cue internal sarcasm.*

"You like to be dominated. I saw a hint of it the second time we had sex. You like when I tell you what to do, when I steal the decisions away from you. I just took it up a notch for tonight."

"I'd say you took it up several notches."

"I guess you're right."

Luke untied my ankles but kept my wrists secured. He knelt in front me, bending my legs so my feet were flat on the bed. When he moved forward, he rubbed his arousal through my folds before positioning himself at my entrance. With his hands on my waist, he pulled me toward him as he thrust inside me. The feeling of his cock and the plug inside me together was an odd sensation, but when he pulled halfway out and pushed back in, the fullness was like no other. I couldn't explain the pleasure, so I stopped trying to dissect it and enjoyed it for what it was.

Undeniable sexual gratification.

He reached for the vibrator, and while the object was dainty, the power it exuded was enough to work me into a frenzy. The pink color surprised me because I couldn't imagine Luke walking into a sex shop and choosing this one. The thought conjured another, and as he slowly worked himself in and out of me, I couldn't hold my tongue. I needed to ask him a question. But he spoke before I could.

"Yes, I bought everything I used on you today brand new. The woman at the shop was extremely helpful. And I thought you'd appreciate the girly color."

"How did you—"

"I may have been gone for years, but I still know you." Out of everything he'd done to me tonight, including him being buried inside me, the last thing he'd said was what made me blush.

198 | S. NELSON

"Now, let's get back to it. I can't wait to hear you scream my name."

And get back to it he did.

He surged inside me so deep I lost my breath completely. I wanted to feel the weight of him on top of me, but he refused to budge from his position, which was him kneeling in front of me. I soon found out why when he placed the head of the vibrator over my clit, circling it around, his hips matching the motion.

"Luke," I moaned, tossing my head to the side in desperation.

"It's starting to happen, isn't it?" All I could do was nod, not wanting to jinx it by verbalizing my answer. "Look at me." I couldn't. I needed to focus, every muscle in my body tightening the closer I got. "Look at me now or I'll stop." That got my attention. When I made eye contact, what I saw pushed me further toward the cliff. The flare of his nostrils as he restrained himself from going faster. The arch of his brow telling me he knew he'd go down in my history as being the man who made me come. The curve of his sexy mouth promising me everything without saying a single word. The heave of his chest and the sheen of sweat coating his skin indicative of the effort he'd given to making sure I was sexually fulfilled.

"I can't... I don't...." I tugged on the soft ropes binding my wrists, wishing I could grab on to him instead. But I remained at his mercy. My entire body vibrating and humming with the need to splinter apart.

Luke rolled my nipple between his fingers, the quick sting of pain driving me closer.

"You're so sexy when you're right there," he praised. "Your skin is flushed, your nipples are hard, and you can barely breathe. I love watching you fall apart." He slammed his hips into mine. "Fuck! I can feel your pussy squeezing me."

I panted his name, trying to take control over what was happening, but I couldn't. I wanted to say so many things, but all other words failed me. I broke with a shudder as relentless waves of pleasure washed over me. My nerve endings were alight as I was held hostage for countless seconds, surrendering to the most exhilarating and intense orgasm of my life. My blood rushed in my veins, my heart beating so fast I could hear the thrumming in my ears. Air was suspended in my lungs as my body continued to fracture into remnants of ecstasy. I arched my back and tried to close my legs, needing to both calm and heighten the throbbing, but Luke held them open, moving his hips at a slow and steady pace as I rode out the last of my climax.

Once the raging pulses subsided and my breathing finally started to regulate, I melted into the bed in a state of utter satiation.

"You're mine now, Olivia," Luke growled, tossing the device to the side and leaning down over me to untie my hands. His mouth was at my ear, the weight of his body on top of me, shoving me out of my moment of enrapture. "A deal is a deal. I made you come and now you're mine." His lips were on mine, kissing me like it would be our last. The way he claimed me was addictive, and the way he moved inside me spurred lingering sensations back to life. "Wrap your legs around me. Perfect." He pulled back and looked deep into my eyes. "Now it's finally my turn." His smile was matched by my own.

The sounds he made were animalistic, filled with longing and need. His moans filled the air, his muscles flexing with every swivel and thrust. He drove into me in long, sure strokes, pinning my hips to the bed as he took what he needed from me. With his face buried in the crook of my neck and my nails raking over his back, he slammed into me one last time so deep I couldn't move if I wanted to. I could feel his heart racing, the slickness of his skin against mine warming me all over. With the slow swivel of his hips, he worked out the last of his orgasm.

"That was incredible."

"I couldn't agree more," I responded. "I knew if we ever made it happen, it would be amazing. But that… that was so much more than I ever dreamed of. I'm still reeling." I stretched my arms to the sides before wrapping them around him, wanting to stay trapped beneath him for hours.

On a long and satisfied sigh, Luke parted his lips once more to speak. "When are you going to tell your mom she doesn't need to fix you up anymore?"

"What do you mean?" I played with him a bit, for my own amusement.

"You're with me now."

I tilted my head in faux confusion, tossing in a frown for good measure. "I'm not understanding."

"What's not to understand?" He lifted himself up, pulled out of me, and rested on his haunches. I wanted to listen to him, to pay attention, but the only thing I could manage was to stare at him, revel in the gloriousness that was Luke Sorenson. But my eyes only made it to his abs when he snapped his fingers and called my name. "You and I are together now. Call it dating or call me your boyfriend. But it means no more going out with other guys. No more kissing anyone else." He looked annoyed when he mentioned that point. "No more pretending you don't like me."

"I wasn't pretending," I clarified. "Not in the beginning, at least. And hold up. Are you telling me you're committing to me, and only me?"

When all he did was stare at me, I thought perhaps he reconsidered making us official, but then he situated himself beside me and pulled me into him. Wrapped up in his arms had quickly become my new favorite position.

"It's only ever been you."

31

LUKE

HAND IN HAND, I LED HER THROUGH MY SIXTY-FIVE-HUNDRED-square-foot rental. She couldn't get over how big the place was as we rounded the corner to yet another bedroom.

"Why would you rent such a large place? What single guy needs five bedrooms and six bathrooms?"

"First off, I'm not single." I squeezed her hand. "Not anymore. And I got it because I enjoy the privacy. Besides, the lake view is amazing."

"You were single when you moved in though." I loved how at every opportunity Olivia didn't try to backpedal. She readily accepted our new status, and I wondered if she believed, as I did, that us ending up together was inevitable.

"I'd rather have too much space than not enough." I did enjoy the expanse of the house, but even I could admit I didn't need all this room. After we were done touring the upstairs, I led her down the staircase and toward the den. The house had come fully furnished—the décor suitable for a guy who didn't have any specific tastes, like me. The light gray color on the walls was uniform throughout, and the dark-stained hardwood floors flowed through every room.

"I'd get lost in here," she gushed, smiling at me as I led her toward the large kitchen. "Wow! I've never seen one so big."

"Are you talking about me or the kitchen?"

She smacked me on the arm before severing our joined hands, running her fingers over the marble countertops.

"This island is gigantic. I wish I had enough room in my kitchen for something half this big."

"The renovations you did on your place are amazing, Ollie. Your place is homey."

"I love my house, but this place is a dream."

"Wanna move in?" I leaned against the nearest wall, waiting for my question to sink in, and for her to react. When I uttered the words, I wasn't sure if I was joking or being serious, but in the seconds that followed, I realized I wanted her to take me up on my offer.

Olivia had been the one who'd gotten away. I still believed I did the right thing all those years ago when I refused to take her virginity because I was leaving for college the following week. But what I regretted was not explaining myself and devising a plan for us to see each other. Hindsight was a bitch, but for as much as I wished to change things, I probably wouldn't be the man I was today if I had. And she wouldn't be the woman I couldn't live without. We did our growing up apart, but I didn't want to waste any more time.

"Yeah, right." She made a face, one that told me she assumed I was joking. I wasn't. When I continued to stare at her, she frowned. "You're kidding, right?"

"No."

"Yes, you are."

"Umm… no, I'm not. Move in with me. You said it yourself, this place is too big for one person."

"I can't move in with you, Luke. That's insane. We've been together for like two seconds." She mumbled something to herself before continuing. "Besides, I have my own house."

SIMPLY COMPLICATED | 203

"Sell it."

"What?"

Her voice raised in surprise, and I could only imagine what she was thinking. I wouldn't deny that I was rushing things, and yes, she was right. We'd established we were together only an hour ago, but I'd wasted ten years not being with her. I wouldn't squander another second.

I was in front of her before she could even think of fleeing my kitchen. "You can put it on the market and move in here."

"No." Her refusal was poised as part statement, part question, but when she said "No" a second time, she was more resolute.

"Why?" I moved closer and linked my hands behind her back, pulling her impossibly close. The need to drag her upstairs was strong. I'd christen every room in this house if she'd let me, but something told me if we didn't hash out the subject we were on, nothing else would be happening any time soon.

"Why?" she parroted. "Because of a million reasons."

"Name some."

"It's too soon. We barely know each other as a couple. I love my house. I'm not selling it. Besides, people will think we're crazy for rushing like this. What if this isn't what you want long term? Then I'll have nowhere to go." A rush of air left her lips. "Disregard the last one. Since I won't be selling my place, the point is moot."

"How about we make another deal."

"No. More. Deals."

"They're so much fun though." I raised the hem of the T-shirt I gave her to wear, gripping the underneath of her ass and picking her up, only to set her on top of the island. Nudging her legs apart, I stepped in between. "If I make you come again, we live together. And since you don't want to leave your place, I could move in with you."

Olivia could deny it, but she contemplated my proposition. But of course, what came out of her mouth was another refusal.

"I said no more deals. And no to moving in together. We can discuss it in the future. Far into the future if we're still together."

"Oh, we'll be together. But how long are you talking?"

"Two years."

Now it was time for my voice to rise. "Two years? That's way too long. How about two months."

"One year," she countered.

"One year?" I grumbled to myself. This woman was insane if she thought I was going to wait that long. "Four months."

"Six."

With narrowed eyes and a breath of hesitation, I agreed. Little did she know we'd be spending all our nights together at either her place or mine. Our belongings would remain separate, but I planned on being with Olivia as much as possible. That being said, I could wait six months to move in with her officially. I'd signed a year lease here, but I'd throw some money at the landlord to get out earlier. Olivia was right, this space was too big. Her house would be perfect for the two of us. But once we started having kids, we'd have to move. Her place was a nice size, with three bedrooms and two bathrooms, but a growing family needed room.

I chose to keep all these thoughts to myself because I didn't know what she'd do if I voiced them. She was still trying to recover from the shock of me asking her to move in together. One word about kids and she might bolt.

"Six months it is." I moved her to the edge of the countertop and removed her shirt as well as my shorts. We were completely naked now, just how I liked it. "Now let's get back to having some fun."

32

OLIVIA

"WHAT DO YOU THINK MARK WILL SAY ONCE HE FINDS OUT ABOUT us?" I asked. We were on the couch, our limbs tangled after having sex for the third time tonight. Round two didn't result in an orgasm for me, but round three did. He'd held me down and used his domineering voice. Not to mention the way he bent me over his lap and swatted my ass multiple times before working me over, this time without the assistance of the vibrator.

"I don't know. We're not kids anymore. It's not like he can forbid me from seeing you like he tried to do before I left."

"What are you talking about?" I raised up on my elbow so I could see his face.

"A week before the incident in my bedroom, when you... you know, I told him I liked you and that I wanted to ask you out. Asked him if he would approve. He flat out told me no, reminding me I was leaving and that wouldn't be fair to you. He was right."

"I love how you two made decisions that involved me, without me." I moved toward the other end of the couch. He tried to snatch my hand to stop me but missed. "He never told me."

"Why would he? He's your brother. He's supposed to protect you, and that's exactly what he did. You were sixteen. He was right to do what he did." I thought about what he said, and we'd agree to disagree. Yes, I was young, but I still should've known about what happened. It would've saved me years of hurt and anger. "I know someone who is going to be thrilled we're together, though."

"My mom?"

"Your mom," he repeated. "She loves me." The smile he wore was infectious, even though I fought to keep mine at bay.

"She doesn't love you that much. Don't get so excited."

"She's like a second mom to me."

"Gross." I laughed as I hopped off the couch, needing to use the bathroom. I didn't get far, though, because Luke was on me, bending over and grabbing me around the backs of my thighs. When he righted himself, he threw me over his shoulder, a move my bladder didn't appreciate.

"I have to pee. Don't jostle me." He ignored me as he hurried toward the stairs. "I'm serious, Luke. You're gonna have a mess if you don't let me down." A smack to my ass told me he wasn't going to release me, so I worked my bladder muscles as best I could until he finally put me down three strides into his bedroom.

"Come here," he growled, reaching for me, but I ran into his bathroom and closed the door, turning the lock right before he tried the handle. A continuous knock made me smile. Someday the same action might irritate me, but for now I allowed myself to live in the moment. Never in a million years did I ever think I'd end up with him. Even while I was angry at him, there was a part of my heart that had always belonged to him. None of the guys I'd dated even compared.

After finishing my business, I swung open the door and there he was, waiting for me.

"I'm horny."

"You're always horny."

"Only for you."

He tugged me into him and kissed me with an intensity I was becoming used to. The only downfall to him ravaging me like this was all I wanted to do was lean into him and forget about everything else. Which I was sure was his plan. But it was late, and I needed to go home. I had early morning appointments I couldn't reschedule just because I wanted to enjoy him until the sun came up.

"Haven't you had enough yet?"

"Not nearly."

He pinned my hands above my head in one of his, using his free hand to glide over my sensitive skin. The brush of his fingers sent a spark through me, and if I didn't stop him now, I never would.

"I have to go," I whispered against his mouth. "I have work tomorrow, and as it is, I'm barely going to get any sleep."

"Stay here."

"I can't. All my stuff is at my house."

"This is exactly why we should move in together. So you can't use these excuses." The curve of his mouth did delicious things to my body, but again, I couldn't indulge.

When I tried to free my hands from his, he tightened his hold. My second attempt proved futile, so the only thing I could think of was to make him, so I raised my knee and pressed it against his balls. I didn't hurt him but applied enough pressure he had no choice but to comply.

"Cheap shot, woman."

"I know."

The sting of his smack on my backside made me yelp, although I should've expected some sort of retaliation. I pulled on my dress, leaving the shredded panties on the floor because they were useless to me now. All that money spent for nothing. Though the pleasure of wearing them and having them ripped from my body because he couldn't wait to see me naked might have been worth it.

"What time do you have practice tomorrow?"

"Nine. Why?"

"Follow me home and spend the night with me." I barely finished speaking before his jeans were yanked up and fastened. The smile on his face deepened as he moved around his bedroom to collect the clothes he'd need for tomorrow.

Staying the night at each other's places was going to be the norm going forward because we were together now. An official couple, although we were the only two privy to the information. Which reminded me, I needed to call Brooke the first chance I got. She'd been team Luke from the beginning.

"I'll get it." Luke walked toward the front door wrapped only in a towel. Not only did I have no idea who had rang the doorbell at seven in the morning, but there was no way he should be greeting whoever was on the other side half naked.

"*I'll* get it."

I rushed past him, managing to grab the handle before he could. When he wouldn't back up to give me room, I turned to look at him, my eyes roaming over him from head to toe. I'd gotten lost in the sight of his gorgeous body when the chime sounded a second time, followed by several raps on the door.

Using my ass to push him back a step, the rich sound of his laughter made me smile, which I was doing a lot of lately. But when he didn't budge from his spot, I pointed back toward the other room, silently telling him I wasn't opening this door until he left. He pouted, which I found endearing. Only when he was out of sight did I open the door. The grin I wore disappeared.

"What are you doing here?"

"Good morning to you, too," Mark said, taking a step inside. "Is that Luke's truck in the driveway?"

"What?" I asked, stalling for time, a tactic which earned me a frown. I wasn't sure how my brother was going to react to the news of me and Luke, and I'd much rather tell him at another time, preferably when the man wasn't sulking around my house in a towel "Um... yes."

"Why is he here?" He took a few more steps toward the other room.

"Why are *you* here?"

"I lent my truck to Stacey. She dropped me off so I could catch a ride into work with you."

"Who's Stacey?"

"Someone I've been seeing."

"I didn't know you were dating anyone."

"I don't tell you everything."

He walked farther into the house and my heart started to race. I had no idea if Luke had gone upstairs, or if he was around the corner. Mark wasn't over-the-top protective to the point where he'd chase away anyone who was interested in me, but finding out his good friend, the same guy he forbade from asking me out years ago, was the one I'd been seeing wouldn't go over too well. Especially with no warning.

In several hurried strides, I blocked him from entering any other room by leaning against the doorway with my arm outstretched.

"Is there something you want to tell me, sis?"

"Who was at the door?" Luke shouted before I could summon an answer for my brother, coming around the corner still wearing only his towel. What was he doing that he couldn't have at least put on clothes?

Even though Mark knew Luke was here, the moment he saw him my stomach dropped.

"Care to tell me what's going on?" His attention bounced from Luke to me and back again. Forcibly moving me aside, he stepped into Luke's personal space. They were pretty much toe to toe, Mark only a hairline shorter than his friend. "Why are you here?" he asked through clenched teeth. It was unfortunate his fists had balled as well.

"I stayed over last night."

"What he means is," I interrupted, "he came over to visit and ended up staying late. I told him he could sleep on the couch, so he didn't have to drive home in the dark." Because I tripped over my words, I had no doubt Mark knew I was lying.

Both men turned to look at me, but it was Luke I focused on. His expression would have been comical had I not been terrified my brother was going to punch him any second.

"That's not what happened at all. I came over here because—"

"Are you two just fucking?"

"Mark!" *Could I be any more embarrassed?*

"No, we're not just fucking. Not anymore, at least."

"Jesus, Luke!" I couldn't believe what either of them were saying, and I'd never been as uncomfortable as I was right now.

Luke walked up next to me and slung his arm over my shoulder, leaned in, and kissed my temple. "We're together. We decided last night."

"Does anyone else know?"

"Not yet," I answered.

"You better tell Mom and soon, because if she gets wind of this before she hears it from you, *I'll* never hear the end of it." Moments passed, and I wasn't sure whether Mark was pissed. He'd asked an inappropriate question, but he didn't yell or threaten Luke. The two men stared at each other and after a small jerk of his chin toward my new boyfriend, Mark's gaze swayed to mine. "I'll meet you outside." He turned to walk away but didn't get far before the other man in the room spoke.

"That's it? You're not going to give me the big-brother speech about how if I hurt your sister, you'll make me regret it?"

"No, because Olivia will be the one to make you regret it. She can handle her own." With his parting words, he walked out my front door, leaving us standing there confused, but relieved the situation never escalated.

"I can't wait to see your mom's reaction."

Luke gripped the steering wheel, and I wondered if he was nervous about telling my parents we were together. He was convinced my mom would be thrilled, which I was sure was going to be the case, but I didn't know how my dad was going to react.

I know he cared for Luke like a second son, but how would he feel about him dating his only daughter? My dad didn't care much for my past boyfriends. He didn't bad mouth any of them when we were dating, but he never went out of his way to get to know them either.

When he pulled into their driveway and shut off the engine, he turned in his seat. His brows were slanted inward, and his teeth toyed with his bottom lip in what I could only assume was anxiousness.

"What's the matter?" I asked.

"Did you tell that guy you're not going to see him again?"

"Derek?" His silence told me the doctor was exactly whom he referred to. Who else would it be? "I didn't even think about it." Truth was, I'd been so caught up in everything that just happened with us, Derek hadn't even entered my mind until he mentioned him.

"Send him a text and tell him you're no longer available."

"You want me to do this right now?" He nodded. "I'll do no such thing. That's rude." He started to object but I cut him off.

"If he reaches out to me again, I'll tell him. But I'm not just going to text him out of the blue."

He pondered what I'd said, but he could take as much time as he wanted. He wasn't going to change my mind.

Luke walked into the house behind me, reaching for my hand as we headed toward the living room. It was past dinner time, and I knew my parents would be watching television. Or at least my mom would be. My dad was probably in the garage working on his vintage Mustang. I called to let them know I was coming over. They didn't know Luke would be with me, though.

"Olivia, is that you?" My mom didn't bother to wait for a response before she started spouting off about the one guy I wish she hadn't, especially with Luke right next to me. "Derek can't stop talking about you, honey. I really think he could be the one." Luke didn't realize how hard he'd squeezed my hand until I smacked his arm. "I'm going to invite him over...." Her words trailed off when she rounded the corner and saw I wasn't alone. "Oh. I didn't know you were coming over, Luke. Mark's not here though." Her attention bounced between us before she glanced down at our clasped hands. The moment she realized Luke was with me and hadn't just stopped over, she smiled so big I thought her cheek muscles surely must've hurt. "Is this what I think it is?"

"What do you think this is?" I asked, loving the brief bout of uncertainty crossing her expression.

"Are you two together?"

"Yes." Luke was the one who answered. "So no more setting her up with anyone. Olivia is all mine now."

She clapped her hands and squealed like this was the best news she'd ever received. "I'm so happy. I have to tell your father." I grabbed her arm before she could run off toward the garage.

"You don't think he'll care, do you?"

"Why would he? He loves Luke."

"I know, but I'm not sure how he'll react to us dating."

She patted my hand. "It'll be fine. He'll be thrilled about it." Her gleeful optimism didn't put my mind at ease like I thought it would.

"What's going on?" My dad rounded the corner, no doubt having heard his wife's scream. My mom grinned like a fool, but my dad had no idea why. "Hey, you two." He looked from us to his wife and back again. "Anyone want to fill me in?"

"They're together," my mom blurted.

"I can see that."

"No, Jack. They're together. Like a couple. They're dating."

His focus turned back to us, his face void of expression when he glanced down at our clasped hands. He walked up to the man next to me in silence.

After a few intense moments passed, my dad placed his arm on Luke's shoulder and said, "It's about time, son."

Both of us exhaled at the same time. "You're not upset?" Luke asked.

"No. I knew you were in love with Olivia before you left for college. I thought you would've made your move then."

"Dad, he wasn't in love with me. We were just friends."

"No, he's right," Luke interjected, turning to look at me. "I was, but because I was leaving, I didn't do anything about it."

"Oh" was all I could say in response. While my words failed me, my pulse sped up, but before my heart threatened to beat out of my chest, I reminded myself that even though he might've been in love with me when we were younger, a concept I was still trying to wrap my head around, it didn't mean that was how he felt about me now.

"Welcome to the family," my dad said, kissing his wife and heading back toward the garage.

"Welcome to the... what?" I looked to my mom first, and when my gaze veered to Luke, the ear-splitting grin on his face warned me he was going to be ridiculous going forward. He'd already broached the subject of moving in together and I could only imagine what ran through his head after he'd basically gotten my father's blessing.

A little while later, after we said goodbye, we walked hand in hand back to his truck. He reached to open my door, but instead of doing so, he spun me around to rest against the side of his vehicle.

"I know this isn't the ideal place to do this, but I can't wait any longer. What I told you inside was the truth. I was in love with you back then, but I kept my feelings to myself because I wouldn't be around, and that wasn't fair to you. If I could go back, I'd do so many things differently. But I can't. What I can do is tell you what I should have ten years ago." He tucked my hair behind my ear and stepped closer. "I love you, Olivia. I have for so long it's part of who I am. *You're* a part of who I am, and I don't want another moment to go by without you knowing. I know you don't feel the same way, but I hope in time you will. Sooner rather than later would be awesome." His grin withered when a tear trickled down my cheek. "Why are you crying?" His shoulders tensed as he studied me.

I barely managed to catch my breath before another tear spilled down my cheek. The thrumming of my heart had started to calm, but now it was back to its frenzied pace.

"You have no idea how many times I dreamed of you saying this to me. I can't believe it's finally happening. And you're wrong. I do feel the same way." His thumb brushed away a third tear. "I love you too."

There was always a piece of me who loved him, even when I was angry with him. And after the first time we kissed in that hotel room, the feelings I'd had for him came back in full force, even though I tried my hardest to deny them and shove them deep down so I didn't have to deal with what they might mean.

Acknowledging I was falling for him all over again meant I'd open myself up to being vulnerable, and I'd worked too hard to toughen up since he'd left.

But now it seemed he'd torn through those walls and had captured my heart once again.

33

LUKE

"ARE YOU OKAY?" BEN ASKED, RUSHING UP NEXT TO ME. "I CAN'T believe Cohen came at you like that."

My argument with him had ended a few days after I punched him for what he said to Olivia. He'd apologized several times, and the only reason I accepted his apology was because I knew what he'd done was out of character. Ever since his woman dumped him, he'd been out of sorts. He asked if he could tell Olivia how sorry he was face to face, but I told him I was more forgiving than her, and to give it more time. Otherwise, I had no idea what she'd say or do. My girl was a spitfire, and I had no doubt she'd hand his ass to him, which he completely deserved.

"I don't know what his problem is."

"He's probably still sore you slept with his girlfriend two years ago." Ben propped his shoulder under my arm and helped me off the field. Eric Cohen played for the Bay City Bucks, the team we were now up against, and he'd always been an asshole, but to sweep my leg as he passed, on purpose because the ball was nowhere near me, was a dick move, regardless of how he felt about me. I'd taken many a tumble during both practices and games, but for some reason it was the way I landed that reaggravated an old injury, an injury that was giving me more trouble these days.

"It was his ex, and I had no idea they'd even dated until he confronted me about it."

Coach approached us, looking none too happy, only this time his displeasure wasn't directed at me.

"Are you hurt?"

"It's my knee." The game was almost over, and we were winning, so it wouldn't be a huge deal for me to sit the rest of it out, but I was pissed he'd caused me any grief at all. A few pain pills and some rest and I'd be good, though.

Thankfully, we weren't the away team today, so I didn't have to worry about traveling for hours to get back home. As I sat on the bench, keeping the weight off my leg, and accepting concern from Andy and Tom, as well as several other of my teammates, I couldn't help but think of Olivia and what I'd told her two nights ago in the driveway of her parents' house.

I didn't want to say those three words to her there, but after admitting to her father that I did in fact love her years ago, I thought it was the best time to tell her I still did.

And to know she felt the same way… I'd be on a high for the rest of my life.

After the game ended, Ben offered to drive me home. I accepted because my knee throbbed, and I didn't want to risk getting into an accident. I shot off a text to Olivia and asked her to meet me there. She'd make me feel better, in more ways than one, I was sure.

Her Jeep was already in the driveway when we pulled up. I'd given her the code to my house, but never told her I hurt my knee or that Ben was driving me home. So when she swung the door open wearing one of the sexy lingerie sets I'd bought her, my eyes almost popped out of my head. And because Ben was on my right, he saw her, which instantly pissed me off. Thankfully, she hadn't been naked because I had no idea what I would've done. Olivia's body was for my eyes only. But if I had to blame anyone for this mishap, it was myself.

Time slowed down right before she shrieked, ducking behind the door so only her head was visible.

"Look away, Mathison," I growled, physically turning his head to the side. He snickered, but I couldn't find anything funny about this situation.

"You didn't tell me someone was going to be with you," she said, still using the big wooden door as a shield.

"I should have. I'm sorry."

"What is *he* doing here anyway?" She looked in Ben's direction, but his head was still turned.

"Can we talk about this after you get dressed, please?"

"Oh. Right."

When the door slammed in our faces, Ben burst out laughing.

"It's not funny."

"It kind of is."

"You can go now. Thanks for the lift. I'll have her give me a ride tomorrow to get my truck." No longer sounding casual, my tone let him know I was still on edge about him seeing her practically naked.

"No worries. Give me your keys. I'll have Tom follow me back tonight. I'll drop it off. Just rest your knee." We didn't have practice the following day, but I was supposed to work out with some of the guys. I supposed that wasn't going to happen now.

Digging my keys out of my pocket, I handed them over, expecting him to leave, but he didn't budge from his spot.

"What are you waiting for?"

"I thought I could apologize to her for what I said."

"I don't think now is such a good time."

"It'll only take a few seconds. I've felt bad ever since it happened, and I need to get rid of this bad karma."

"Like I said, I don't—"

Before I could finish speaking, Olivia opened the door, this time dressed in shorts and a plain black shirt. She was all covered up, but I knew what she had on underneath. And so did Ben.

I opened my mouth to tell her that he wanted to apologize for how he acted, but he started talking before I could get a word out.

"Olivia, I wanted to tell you how sorry I am for what I said to you. I was out of line and it was inappropriate."

She cast her narrowed eyes toward him, wearing no other expression. Was she going to be pissed at me for basically ambushing her? Because that wasn't my intention at all.

"You think?" She wore her sass like a badge, and I loved her even more for it.

"I was an asshole."

"I'm not arguing with you," she said, looking at me before turning her attention back to him.

"Again, I'm really sorry. I hope you can forgive me."

When she opened her mouth again, I held my breath. I had no idea if she was going to tell him off or accept his apology. She could go either way, and no matter what she said to him, I'd support her one hundred percent.

Her shoulders bounced in a lazy shrug. "I guess I understand why you were such a jerk to me. I mean, it's not really your fault, I guess." My buddy and I shared a confused glance. "Luke filled me in on your 'issue,'" she said, using air quotes on the last word.

"My issue?" Ben's voice displayed his confusion.

She leaned in close like she was about to reveal a secret. "He told me you have a little dick and that's why you act inappropriate sometimes." The corner of her mouth twitched, and I about lost it once her words hit their mark.

Ben's eyes widened right before he swiveled his focus on me.

His mouth opened and closed several times before he finally found his words.

"I don't know what he told you, but I don't have a little dick. I don't," he emphasized before pointing at me. "You know I don't. You've seen it in the shower."

"I'm sorry. He didn't say *little* dick. He said *tiny* dick. I was being generous by saying little." Olivia's face scrunched up as if she were truly having an honest and uncomfortable conversation. When in reality, she was rightfully giving him a dig, even though it wasn't true. But I wasn't going to clarify anything for him. He deserved this.

"I gotta go, buddy," I said, taking two steps into the house.

"Tell her it's not true, man," he demanded as I closed the door on him. He spouted off a few choice expletives before walking down the front steps.

"He deserved that." Olivia threw her arms around my neck. "If there's one thing I know about guys, it's that their dick means everything to them. Insult their manhood and they can't get over it." Several seconds passed before she spoke again. "Sorry for answering the door in my underwear. I didn't know you'd have anyone with you."

"No need to apologize. That was my fault, and believe me, I'm kicking myself for it."

"Thank God I didn't answer the door naked. Can you imagine?"

"No. Because I would've been forced to pluck his eyes out, and he's no good to the team blind."

"You're so dramatic." She leaned up on her tiptoes to kiss me, but before our mouths connected, she pulled back. "Wait, why did he bring you home? Where's your truck?"

Apparently, she hadn't seen me struggling to keep weight off my right leg.

"I hurt my knee at the game, so he gave me a lift."

"Oh no. Are you all right? Are you in a lot of pain?"

"It's more of a throbbing, but I'll be okay."

"Let me help you to the couch." She placed her shoulder under my arm like Ben had earlier, only this position was a little more cumbersome because I was taller. But we managed to make it to the sofa without incident. "What do you need?"

"You. Out of those clothes. Now."

"Seriously?"

"I'm not joking." I snapped my fingers at her, which only served to earn me a tiny scowl. But I was persistent. "Now, woman."

"You're lucky I love you," she said, smiling as she slowly stripped off her clothes.

"Trust me. I know."

34

OLIVIA

"You look fantastic." Luke circled me, running his hand over my backside before giving my cheek a squeeze. "Damn, woman. I don't think I want to take you to Heather's wedding now. I just want to stay in and ravage you."

Because I agreed to accompany him today, he insisted on purchasing my dress. The gorgeous shade of maroon made my green eyes pop. The hemline reached midcalf and was slightly longer in the back than in the front, the bottom several inches of sheer material. The neckline dipped into a respectable V, and a stunning, silver-beaded detailed broach sat directly below the bustline.

"I'm sure your sister and parents won't appreciate that too much. Besides, aren't you in the wedding party?"

When he stepped in front of me, he grabbed me by the waist and pulled me close, tipping my head upward so he could look into my eyes. He liked to do that a lot. Sometimes it was because he wanted me to pay extra attention to what he said, and sometimes he was silent. I didn't mind one bit, however, because I easily lost myself in his beautiful, soul-searching gaze.

"Not anymore. They made changes last minute and now

only have a best man and a matron of honor. Which is fine with me. The less I have to do, the better." He smiled but the expression wasn't completely genuine.

I'd gotten good at deciphering his moods, as he did mine. "What's the matter?" I rested my hand on the side of his clean-shaven face. I loved when Luke wore a bit of scruff, but this look was just as sexy.

"Nothing."

"Are you sure?" I asked, skeptical he wasn't telling me the truth. Glancing down at his knee, I thought perhaps it was bothering him. "Are you in pain?"

"No." His mouth covered mine and the tip of his tongue teased my bottom lip. When I opened for him, he pulled back. "I...." His eyes shifted downward, the silence making my heart pick up its pace because he was acting a little strange. "I'm consumed with the way I feel about you, and sometimes it scares me. I've never been in this situation before. Not with anyone else. There are times I think I'm going to lose my mind with all the irrational fears I have whenever I look at you. I know you're mine now, but that can change at any moment."

The desperation in his stare warmed my heart, making me realize we shared the same affliction. I was often bombarded with the fear that he would change his mind about me, realize he didn't love me, and he'd come to recognize what we had was nothing more than passing lust. I feared he would one day view me as not enough and move on.

There were women vying for his attention everywhere he went, even while I stood beside him. They were brazen and looking to hook up with him, even if only for a one-time deal. Temptation was all around him, and because of who he was, I tended to have quite a few jealous moments, each time him reassuring me he had no interest in anyone other than me.

"Are you afraid I'm going to leave you, or that you'll change your mind about me?" I asked cautiously.

"I'd never leave you." He linked his hands behind my back. "I love you way too much. I never want to picture my life without you."

"Then don't. Because you're stuck with me now."

"Promise?"

"I do."

Luke took a step forward, causing me to follow suit as I took a step back. Within only a few strides, the bed brushed up against the backs of my knees.

"I have to say, I love hearing those two words come out of your mouth." He tried to push me onto my back, but there was no way I was going to let him ruin all the work I'd done with my dress and my hair, which was styled in perfect waves. I shoved at his shoulder to get him to back up, but he didn't budge.

I refused to acknowledge what he'd said, though. It'd barely been a month since he brought up the topic of moving in together, I wasn't going to broach the subject of marriage.

"Luke," I said in warning, all while the corners of my mouth tipped upward. This man was too gorgeous and sexy for his own good, especially while sporting a black suit. "We're not having sex right now. You're going to have to wait until later." With more might this time, I managed to persuade him to retreat a few steps. Smoothing down the bottom of my dress, I stepped around him.

"How about you put your hands against the wall, and I take you from behind? That way I won't mess up your dress or your hair?" The slow tip of his lips excited me, and I contemplated his offer, but in the end, us losing ourselves to each other would make us late. When we did have sex, I didn't want to rush. I wanted to take my time and enjoy my man.

"Not going to happen." With my denial, I raised the bottom of my dress, allowing him to peek at the black lacy thong I'd donned for the occasion. "Besides, I really like these, and I don't want you to rip them in your frenzy of horniness." I did a little twirl, and when my back was to him, a few choice expletives flew from his mouth.

He really was an ass man.

"Why am I so nervous all of a sudden? It's not like I don't know your family."

I'd known Luke's family practically my entire life, but when his parents moved four years ago, I'd only run into his mother once at the post office, almost two years back.

"I have no idea," he answered, reaching over to grab my hand, giving it a gentle squeeze. His comfort went a long way to help settle my sudden bout of nerves. "When was the last time you saw my sister?"

"I ran into her a little less than a year ago. She was with John at the time, so I got to meet him. He seems nice."

"He's okay."

His response was unexpected because I was under the impression he liked his soon-to-be brother-in-law. He'd never made any comments to the contrary. To me, anyway.

"You don't like him?"

His head swiveled toward me. "I said he was okay." When I returned his stare in silence, he elaborated. "He's marrying my little sister. He's not good enough for her, but no one is. Compared to her other boyfriends, though, John is the best choice. So… he's okay."

"Good thing Mark doesn't feel that way about you," I joked, but my jovial expression disappeared when he grimaced.

"Trust me. He does."

"No, he—"

"Yes, he does," he interrupted. "Every man who loves his sister feels the same way. Just because Mark didn't start yelling when he found out about us doesn't mean he feels any different than I do about John. Mark sees me as the better option compared to your other boyfriends, and from what you've told me about your last one, I'm going to have to agree."

"There's no comparison at all."

"That better be in my favor," he teased.

"Of course."

My anxiousness had all but dissipated until we pulled into the parking lot of the church, which was located forty-five minutes from my house. I was back to feeling uneasy. I couldn't readily pinpoint why the emotion overtook me. It could be because this would be the first time we'd see his family as a couple. I'd always gotten along well with his parents, and even though Heather was a year younger than me, and we ran in different circles in high school, we'd always been friendly toward each other. But knowing them as my neighbors once upon a time, and now seeing them again as Luke's girlfriend might be why I'd been hit with a case of the worries.

"Get out of your head, Olivia. Whatever you're thinking, stop."

"Do they know I'm coming with you today?" Our hands were clasped as he led me toward the church steps. As we walked by, a few of the people milling around outside whispered and pointed when they saw him. Some even approached and told him they were a big fan of his.

"I thought I'd surprise them." I tugged back on my arm, but his hold only tightened. He laughed. "I'm kidding. Yes, they know you're coming. They're fully aware we're together and they're excited to see you. Stop worrying they'll think you're only after me because of my money."

"I wasn't thinking that, but now I am."

He leaned in close to whisper in my ear. "I'll tell them you're using me for sex." Before I could react, he kissed me, and I could feel him smile against my lips.

"Not funny," I mumbled against his mouth, hoping he'd never tell anyone else about how we hooked up. I'd have to make him promise to take that one to his grave.

The beautiful ceremony and reception were held outside at the Glen Morrow Country Club, under an enormous white tent. There had to be at least twenty round tables spread throughout the space, each one accommodating ten guests. The head table seated the four people in the bridal party, along with the matron of honor's husband and the best man's wife.

Opulence was in abundance. There were numerous chandeliers hanging from the ceiling of the tent, and countless candles lit throughout. The centerpieces were huge flower balls of white roses. A makeshift bar had been set up along the length of the right side of the tent, as well as a secondary one outside. Several tables were available for guests who wanted to enjoy the cocktail hour in the sunshine.

Luke stayed by my side, exchanging pleasantries with those who wished to fawn over him. Thankfully, they were respectful enough not to linger too long, realizing this was his sister's wedding and he wanted to enjoy himself.

I'd spoken with his sister, her new husband, and Luke's parents at the church after the ceremony. They were as friendly and as loving as I remembered, telling me how thrilled they were I was the one who ended up snagging Luke. When he told them he was the one who snagged me and not the other way around, my heart filled with even more love for the man.

Thirty minutes into the cocktail hour, Luke asked if I'd be all right for a few minutes while he visited with some people he hadn't seen in a few years. I sent him on his way with a kiss and told him to take his time, assuring him I would be fine.

I should've asked if I could accompany him, however,

because the second he was free of me, a black-haired woman wearing a green dress that barely covered her ass, sidled up next to him. I'd caught her ogling him earlier but didn't say anything because I didn't want to come across as insecure. The hussy pawed at him, and even though Luke backed away from each one of her advances, I couldn't help but wonder if he liked the attention.

Yeah, that was where my head went.

Her breasts were on display and there was no way he hadn't noticed. I'd seen them yards away. Seeing what she had, self-consciousness of my smaller chest rolled through me. Luke was an ass man, but every guy liked big boobs, right? And I didn't think the bitch had fake ones either.

Lost to my own inner torture, I was unaware someone stood behind me at the outside bar. I'd placed an order for a glass of red wine, and as the bartender slid the glass across the wooden top, someone bumped into me. Luckily, I hadn't picked up my drink yet because I would've spilled it for sure.

"Excuse me."

"No problem," I responded, turning to see who the culprit was, and as soon as I saw him, I wished I were anywhere else.

"Olivia? What are you doing here?" Cody asked, his gaze scaling the length of me. He inched closer, the corners of his eyes crinkling. There was a time I believed that smile had been reserved for me. As I stared back at him, in his light gray suit, complete with a pink tie, I couldn't believe I was once in love with him. Or at least I believed I was at one point. His dark blond hair was shorter than it was four months ago.

"I'm here as someone's date." I didn't want to say who because my ex was a fan of Luke, having been obsessed with the game as long as we'd been together. I never told him I knew his favorite player, though, mainly because at the time I didn't want to talk about him, and Cody would be relentless with the questions.

His lingering attention made me take a step back. "You look fantastic." His finger trailed down my arm and once his touch registered, I moved back another step until his hand fell away. "Did you look this good when we were together?"

I wanted to say, "Maybe if I did, you wouldn't have cheated on me," but that would be me accepting some of the unrealistic blame for him acting like a selfish, self-centered, grade-A asshole. And I wasn't about to shoulder any of the responsibility for his actions. Besides, his question was insulting, to say the least.

"What are you doing here?" I asked, hoping the deflection would work.

"I'm friends with John, the groom. We went to high school together." *This world is too small sometimes.*

"Did you come with anyone?"

I refused to let him know I was aware he had a girlfriend, or at least he did the last time I was on his Facebook page, which was before I started up with Luke.

"My girlfriend."

"That's nice."

"Is it?"

"What do you mean?"

He shrugged, taking another step closer, invading my personal space. "Don't you miss me?"

There was something about the way he looked at me that reminded me of when I'd first been interested in him. I thought he was so handsome, with his perfect teeth and chiseled features. But as it turned out, I preferred guys who didn't cheat on me, and treat me as if I'd done something wrong to assuage their own guilt.

"No, I don't."

"There was a time when we were good together."

He reached for my hand, but I took a step back, turning to see if I could locate Luke. I needed to be saved from Cody because I didn't want to make a scene, and I feared if I spent any more time with this jerk, a spectacle was exactly what was going to happen.

Luke stood near the other end of the bar, and he must've sensed my distress because his eyes met mine almost immediately. He winked at me, but when my eyes widened and my lips formed a strained line, he frowned. Seconds later, he caught sight of Cody standing too close, and his nostrils flared, the crease between his brows becoming more defined.

I turned back around confident I'd been able to silently beckon my boyfriend to come and rescue me.

"We were never good together. That would imply you treated me with respect, which you didn't."

He chuckled, as if my statement was ludicrous. And when he parted his lips to say something else, he looked over my head, his jaw practically hitting the floor. I had no doubt my man was walking this way. A breath of relief left my body, and the second Luke grabbed my waist and pulled me into him, I smiled. If I wanted to get back at Cody for cheating on me and treating me like crap for the last few months of our relationship, this was exactly what would do the trick.

Luke had no idea who Cody was. He probably just figured it was some guy hitting on me. How would he react once he found out this was someone I dated before him? I'd initially beckoned him over to save me because I didn't want to cause a scene, but I might've inadvertently caused a situation that would result in some sort of incident anyway, having no idea what Luke would do or say.

"Luke Sorenson. How are you?" Cody extended his hand and Luke took it. "I'm a big fan."

"Thanks, man." Luke severed the greeting and leaned in to kiss my temple. "Are you hitting on my woman?" Luke's smile was deceptive because although he appeared friendly and as if he was teasing Cody, he was annoyed. I knew him well enough to tell from the plunge in his tone.

Cody's eyes swung back to mine. "You're here with him?"

"Yes. He's my boyfriend."

"When did you... how do you even know him?" My ex looked upset, and I didn't know if it was because I was with someone else and not fawning over him, or because he hadn't been aware I knew his favorite player. But at this point, I didn't care.

But to dig the knife in even more, I said, "Luke is an old family friend whom I've reconnected with."

"And now we're together." Luke's fingers dug into my waist in either a show of possession or confusion as to who Cody was. By now, he could tell I knew the guy, simply by the familiar way in which he spoke to me. "And how do you know Olivia?"

Cody cleared his throat first before answering. "We used to date."

"Really?"

"Cody was the guy I dated before you," I added, leaning back into Luke for comfort.

"*This* is Cody?"

"Why do you say it like that?" My ex went from fawning over Luke to looking at him with utter annoyance.

"Didn't you cheat on her?"

"It was all a misunderstanding." He tried to save face or lie or spin the reality of what he did into his warped version, but I knew the truth, a truth I'd told Luke all about.

Luke leaned in close to my ear but spoke loud enough for Cody to hear. "Isn't this the guy you said was lousy in bed?"

My surprised expression was enough to let Cody know I'd said something to Luke about his lack of skill in the sack. I never said he was lousy, because he had tried to please me in the beginning of our relationship, but Luke obviously knew I never had an orgasm with the guy.

"You said I was a bad lay?" Before I could answer, he spouted off, "Maybe if you weren't impossible to please, you would've had more fun."

"Impossible?" Luke asked, his voice dipping even lower than before. "Seems to me like you didn't know what you were doing."

Cody slinked off soon after, snatching the wrist of a bleached blonde who was talking with a group of men. Once he was out of sight, I turned and threw my arms around Luke's neck, leaning up on my tiptoes.

"That was both embarrassing and awesome." When I pressed my lips to his, he took my mouth in a panty-melting kiss. I didn't care there were other people around. All I wanted to do was be consumed by this man. When I finally pulled back, in need of some air, his grin made my heart skip a beat.

"That was fun."

"It was."

"I'm happy you're not mad at me for saying what I did."

"If it was anyone else, I might be, but he's someone who deserves to be called out and embarrassed."

"What if your sister hadn't been getting married?" I blurted as we stood in the middle of his bedroom, preparing to turn in for the night. I left out parts of my thought process without intending to, eager to hear his answer, even though he probably didn't have a clue as to what I was talking about.

"What do you mean?"

"After the first time we had sex. What if you didn't need a date to Heather's wedding? Do you think we still would've continued hooking up?"

"Hooking up?" He clearly wasn't a fan of the phrase, if his frown was any indication. He walked up behind me and moved my hair to the side, grabbing the zipper of my dress and parting the material. "After that first time, there was no way I was going to let you go. I would've thought of something. It just so happens my sister was the perfect excuse."

"I'm sure she'd be thrilled to hear that."

"Nah. I think we'll keep that tidbit of information to ourselves." He kissed the back of my neck, shoving the dress farther down my body until it pooled at my feet. I stepped out and turned to face him. "You're so beautiful."

"And you're sweet." When he reached to pull me closer, I retreated, just out of reach. Tapping my finger against my lips, hungry for his dominant side, I said, "But I don't want sweet right now."

"You don't?" The slight arch of his eyebrow told me he was on board. "What do you want?"

"I want you to control me. Do whatever you want to me, however you want to do it." I spun around, peering at him over my shoulder, my satin thong exposing his favorite asset of mine. "Start with reddening my ass."

Expletives flew from his mouth as he adjusted his growing erection. In a single stride, he managed to seize my waist, but instead of tugging me closer, he pushed me against the wall.

"Don't move."

The rustle of his clothes echoed around the room as he stripped down. The heat of his naked body warmed mine when he pressed his chest to my back, gripping my throat from behind, his lips resting near my ear. But he didn't say anything, instead tapping the outside of my thigh. I spread my legs. A tug on my earlobe with his teeth thanked me for my submission.

"I love you." My words took flight on a whisper, but he heard me loud and clear.

He rubbed the tip of his cock through my silky wetness, hitting against my clit several times and stealing my breath.

"Say it again," he demanded, twisting me back around. When

our eyes connected, I fell into them, wanting a bit of sweet after all.

"I love you," I repeated, sighing with relief Luke was finally all mine.

"I love you more, baby." A glint of excitement permeated the tender look he cast my way, the steel set of his jaw bringing forth the side of him I'd asked for. "Do you want me to make you come?"

"Always."

He took a step back and fisted his arousal. "On your knees." The rasp in his voice sent a shiver of exhilaration through me. The soft plushness of the carpet cradled my knees as I got into position. With my hands on the deep-cut V of his abdomen, I moved to take him into my mouth, but he tipped my head upward, peering so deeply into my eyes I swore he saw my soul. "Promise me this won't stop once we're married."

"I prom—wait—what?"

Instead of answering, he jerked his hips forward and licked his lips. "Open." I didn't, needing clarification on his out-of-the-blue statement. The only thing shaking my head did, though, was make the corners of his mouth kick up. "Now, Olivia, or I'll bring you to the edge repeatedly and won't allow you to come." His seductive threat was enough to make me comply.

An hour later, after a mind-blowing orgasm, we lay tangled in each other's arms, our limbs entwined as our chests rose and fell in unison. Sleep beckoned, but I wanted to discuss something he'd said earlier.

"Can we talk about what you said before?"

He cradled me closer. "Sure."

"You're not going to ask what I'm talking about?"

"No. I was fully aware that when I mentioned marriage you

were going to get all weirded out. It's the same response you had when I suggested we move in together, which by the way is now only one hundred and fifty-eight days away."

I propped myself up on my elbow. "I said we could talk about moving in together in six months, not that we were going to do it then."

He mirrored my position, throwing his leg over mine and yanking me forward. His arousal stabbed me in the belly. He was ready to go again, but we weren't doing anything until we finished this conversation.

"No." He shook his head vigorously. "Six months. I agreed to that timeframe. We're not talking about it. We're doing it."

"But I don't—"

"You overthink too much, Ollie." His nickname for me irritated me less and less each time he uttered it, and I believed it was because now I knew he truly loved me, and he wasn't solely trying to get under my skin to irritate me.

"I know, but still." *That's my argument?*

"You're it for me. I don't want anyone else. Ever. Do you feel the same, or are you unsure?" His breathing stalled as he waited for my reply.

"Yes." The hesitant grin he wore fell and I hated he'd misunderstood me. "Yes, I feel the same way. And no, I'm not unsure about us. You're it for me too."

His cheeks puffed up right before he exhaled. "You scared me."

"Sorry."

"And because you did," he said, rolling on top of me and spreading my legs with his knee so he could nestle in between, "you're going to have to make it up to me."

"What did you have in mind?" My head came up off the pillow to capture his mouth, but he pulled back.

"Agree to be mine forever." The sexiest smile spread across his face, and it took a moment for his words to register.

"What are you saying?"

"I'm saying I want you to agree to be mine. For as long as we both shall live."

"That sounds like a marriage vow. Or at least, a proposal." I wanted to put some distance between us because him on top of me was too much of a distraction for me to think clearly. I wanted to shout "Yes" to everything he'd said, but I didn't want to rush anything either.

"Stop freaking out. I'm not proposing. Yet."

"You're not?"

Why was I disappointed? Oh, no. This man had me so twisted up I couldn't land safely on any side. Did I want to move in with him sooner than I said? Yes. No. Did I want to be engaged to him right now? No. Yes.

"No. But I'm giving you notice, I will be. So be prepared."

After taking some of the longest seconds of my life to ponder the best response, one I wanted to give and one he'd want to hear, I parted my lips and gave life to five words.

"I look forward to it."

epilogue

LUKE

Eighteen Months Later

I HAD TO REMIND MYSELF NOT TO FOCUS ON ANYTHING BUT THE game. We were playing the Miami Mavericks, my old team, and while I was friends with most of the players, they were now my opponents. I wasn't going to go easy on them. Not one bit, especially today.

I'd been playing professional soccer for the past ten years, signing at only twenty years old, but I'd been playing the game since I was four. And after much deliberation, talking to my parents, to Olivia, and to my coach, I decided six months ago to retire. Today was my last game.

Up until a month ago I'd had mixed feelings about my decision. Some days I was confident with my choice, and other days I'd thought I'd made a mistake. On those days Olivia would listen to me vent and remind me that it was time to move on and to do something else, which was coaching. I still wanted to be involved in soccer, I just didn't want to play it professionally any longer.

I hated to admit this, but I wasn't young anymore, not for the sport, at least. My body had taken a beating over the years. Between the constant training, the practices, the games, and the injuries, I'd had enough. I wanted to be able to run after our kids whenever we decided it was time to start a family.

Ben jogged up next to me, smiling big when he tapped his wrist. That was his indication the first half of the game was almost over.

"You sure about this, man?" he asked, coming to stand on my left.

"Absolutely." My heart thrashed inside my chest, and I became nauseous, but excitement battled to the forefront.

When I glanced behind me, Tom and Andy grinned, knowing what was coming in the next few minutes.

It was the reason I made sure my and Olivia's families were in attendance today, as well as Brooke, who was like Olivia's sister. She'd also brought her girlfriend, Kate. I wasn't going to be shy about one more person as a witness. I had twenty thousand in the stands and probably millions watching on television. It was widely publicized this was my final game. But I couldn't think about the pressure to play my absolute best, which I would, or the countless pairs of eyes that would be watching what I had planned, because I knew they would be.

I took it one second at a time, and when the referee blew the whistle to indicate the first half was finished, the urge to throw up again hit me hard. But I kept myself together.

Tom came up behind me and slapped me on the back. "Deep breaths."

Next it was Andy. He bumped my shoulder with his. "I don't envy you." He laughed as he walked toward the side of the field.

"Don't listen to him," Ben said. "You're one lucky guy, Luke. I'm jealous." Squeezing my shoulder, he jogged off to join the others.

Coach looked at me, and when I nodded, he produced a microphone. When I approached him about helping me out with my plan, he was only too happy to assist. All the players were off the field at this point, and the fans who'd gotten up from their seats sat back down once he started to speak.

"As all of you know, today is Luke Sorenson's last game." There was a collective groan, which I had to admit made me feel good. "And he wanted to do something special during his last halftime." I walked up next to him right before he started speaking again. "Will Olivia Brighton please come down to the field?" Coach threw his arm around my shoulder and pulled me in for a quick half-hug embrace. "Good luck. And remember not to focus on anything but her."

As soon as he walked away, my stomach flipped, and my pulse thrummed loudly in my ears. Both of our families were seated near the field, so I had Olivia in my sights.

It took her a few seconds to realize it was her name that Coach called, and when she did, she didn't move, staring at everyone seated next to her before finally looking in my direction. I'd already chatted with Mark about what was going to happen. In fact, they all knew, and had thankfully not uttered a word to her. But it was Mark whom I wanted to bring her down in case she got embarrassed and didn't want to walk to the field alone. Which was what happened. Her brother got her to her feet and grabbed her hand. He didn't drag her to me, but his hurried steps urged her to follow.

Once they were near, he shook my hand, and kissed his sister's cheek before heading back to the stands.

"What's going on?" she asked, keeping her eyes on me. "Why did he call me down here?"

I reached for the hand that Mark had released, which happened to be her left, and slowly lowered to one knee.

OLIVIA

Sitting in the stands watching Luke play had my stomach in knots. This game was unlike any other because it was his last. I didn't want him to have any regrets about how he played, and I also didn't want him to get injured either. I didn't think his poor knee could take much more, although he assured me this morning, he was fine.

The man had skills, never mind he looked amazing while on the field. All his fancy footwork and precision with the ball were just two of the things that made him worth every dollar they paid him. But unfortunately, I wasn't the only one who noticed. He had his own cheering section, and most of them were women, vying for a glimpse from him.

I'd been able to tamp down some of my jealousy where his female fans were concerned, knowing how much he loved me, but once in a while, the green-eyed monster would rear its ugly head. During those times, I'd remind myself I was the one he came home to every single day. Speaking of, Luke moved into my house a year ago. Compared to the place he rented, I didn't think he'd be satisfied with the smaller size, even though my house was by no means tiny. But he preferred the homey feel over the cold bachelor pad he'd been living in. We did, however, have plans to add an addition. He told me it was for a home gym and extra guest bedroom, but I caught him looking up pictures of nurseries on his phone. I didn't say a word to him about it, though. While I wasn't ready to have kids yet, I loved that he was looking to our future, wanting to build a family with me.

"This is so exciting," Brooke said, leaning into me. "I can't believe it took me this long to come and see him play. He's amazing."

"He is," I said proudly. "But nothing like waiting until the last minute. You're lucky you caught his last game."

All Luke knew was playing soccer, but I agreed when he said

life was too short and he wanted to step back and do something else with the sport. He'd be a wonderful coach whenever he tackled that role.

I was in midchat with Brooke and Kate when the ref blew his whistle. The first half had ended, and when I happened to look toward the field, the only two people left out there were Luke and his coach, who happened to now be holding a microphone.

Was this a surprise tribute to him for his retirement? Or did Luke know about this? And if so, why didn't he mention anything to me?

My best friend squeezed my arm, and I assumed it was because she was excited for whatever was going to happen for my man.

With my eyes glued to Luke, mesmerized with the mere sight of him, my name being spoken didn't register at first. But when Mark stood and reached for my hand, I instinctually took it, even though I wasn't sure what was going on.

When we were several yards away from the field, Luke shifted from one foot to the other several times, his eyes pinned to mine the entire time. When we were close enough, my brother dropped my hand, shook Luke's, kissed my cheek, and walked back to where our families sat.

"What's going on?" I asked once we were alone, or as alone as we could be with a stadium filled with people. "Why did he call me down here?"

Without a response, Luke placed my left palm in his and slowly lowered himself to one knee. The sight of him in that position made my heart speed up, warmth spreading over every part of my body. Hearing his voice brought me back to the moment, and it didn't take long before my free hand covered my mouth and my eyes welled with unshed tears.

"Olivia, I've thought about how to do this since the day I mentioned wanting us to move in together, which seems like forever ago now. I was going to do it on our one-year anniversary, but we hadn't been living together long and I knew you'd be hesitant to take this step. You'd say it was too fast and I didn't want you to feel rushed. So, I waited, and waited. But I can't wait any longer. I'm closing one chapter of my life and want to start another. With you. I love you so much. You make me happier than I ever thought I could be, and if you'll let me, I'll try to make you feel the same every day for the rest of our lives." He opened the top of a ring box, took a deep breath through his nose, and released the air through his mouth. His nerves were on par with mine. "Will you marry me?"

When I stared into his eyes, the love I had for him was reflected back at me. There wasn't an ounce of hesitation when I removed my hand from my mouth and let my arm drop to my side, my lower lip quivering as a single tear trailed down my cheek.

"Yes."

I wanted to say so much more, but I only produced enough sound to give life to one word.

Luke stood, placed the biggest princess-cut diamond I'd ever seen on my finger, and wrapped his arms around me. Our kiss was far from PG-13, but right now I didn't care who saw.

Even though there were thousands of witnesses and probably millions watching from home, this moment between us seemed private. No one could hear what he'd said except me, and while I wanted to push him to the field and ravage him, give him a taste of what he was in for later tonight, I restrained myself, albeit barely.

As we walked hand in hand toward our families, hearing the cheers from the fans and knowing they shared in our excitement, I leaned into the man I'd loved since I was a teenager. And although he'd been gone for a decade, my feelings hadn't changed. I pretended they had, disguising the love with anger, and hurt, but the moment I saw him sitting next to me at

McConley's, everything I'd shoved deep down had started to blossom again.

I fought it.

I tried to deny I felt anything for him.

But he was persistent, chipping away at the armor I'd built around my heart. He managed to make me fall even harder for him than before.

Accepting his offer to help me with my dilemma had been the best decision I ever made. And because of it, I was now the luckiest woman in the world because Luke was all mine.

Forever and always.

THE END

WANT A STORY THAT WILL LEAVE YOU BREATHLESS?
THEN GRAB YOUR COPY OF ADDICTED, BOOK ONE IN
THE ADDICTED TRILOGY

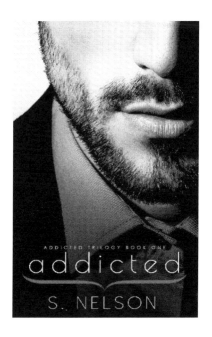

She intrigues him.
She challenges him.
She threatens the secret he's been hiding for years.
Will a promise made long ago be the very same thing that
destroys their chance for happiness?

IF YOU'RE LOOKING FOR A BINGE WORTHY MC READ
THAT WILL CONSUME YOU, THEN START TODAY WITH
MAREK

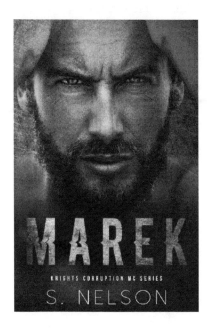

With the weight of the club on his shoulders, Cole Marek,
president of the Knights Corruption MC, had only one choice:
Turn their livelihood legit.
Everything was falling into place until one unexpected, fateful
night. With an attack on his fellow brothers, Marek had no
choice but to retaliate against their sworn enemy.
Swarming their compound, he comes face-to-face with the
daughter of his rival club, making an astonishing decision
which would change his life forever.

STAY INFORMED

Did you enjoy Simply Complicated?

Want to find out about S. Nelson's next novel?

Each month she sends out updates on upcoming books, sales, cover reveals, and awesome giveaways.

Get her FREE monthly newsletter by going to:
www.subscribepage.com/snelsonnewsletter

About the Author

S. Nelson grew up with a love of reading and a very active imagination, never putting pen to paper, or fingers to keyboard until 2013.

Her passion to create was overwhelming, and within a few months she'd written her first novel. When she isn't engrossed in creating one of the many stories rattling around inside her head, she loves to read and travel as much as she can. She lives in the Northeast with her husband and two dogs, enjoying the ever-changing seasons.

If you would like to follow or contact her, please feel free to do so at the following:

Website: www.snelsonauthor.com
Email: snelsonauthor8@gmail.com

Also on Facebook, Goodreads, Amazon, Instagram, Twitter, BookBub and TikTok

Note to Reader

If you are a new reader of my work, thank you so much for taking a chance on me. If I'm old news to you, thank you for continuing to support me. It truly means the world to me.

If you've enjoyed this book, or any of my other stories, please consider leaving a review. It doesn't have to be long at all. A sentence or two will do just fine. Of course, if you wish to elaborate, feel free to write as much as you want.

Acknowledgments

Thank you to my husband for being patient with me as I lock myself away in my office for countless hours. Thank you for giving me the time I needed to get these characters out of my head and onto paper. I love you!

Becky, thank you so much for pushing me. I need to take a breather after I read your comments, lol, but your suggestions and insight are what helps me to polish the story and make it the best it can be.

Clarise at CT Cover Creations. Your work speaks for itself. I'm absolutely thrilled with this book cover. It's beyond gorgeous!

Ruth, I truly don't know what I'd do without you. Scratch that, yes, I do. I'd go crazy. I'm beyond grateful to have you in my corner. I look forward to our chats and love that you love my men as much as I do.

To all the bloggers who have shared my work, I'm forever indebted to you. You ladies are simply wonderful!

To all of you who have reached out to me to let me know how much you loved my stories, I am beyond humbled. Thank you so much, and I'll continue to do my best to bring you stories you can lose yourself in, even if it's only for a few hours.

And last but not least, I would like to thank you, the reader. If this is the first book you've read from me, I hope you enjoy it. If this is yet another story from me you've taken a chance on... THANK YOU from the bottom of my heart!

S. Nelson

reading order list

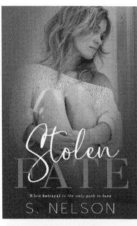
Stolen
FATE
When betrayal is the only path to love
S. NELSON

A light in the darkness
REDEMPTION
S. NELSON

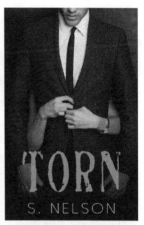
TORN
S. NELSON

Blind
DEVOTION
S. NELSON

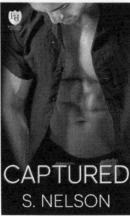
CAPTURED
S. NELSON

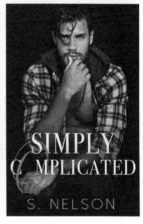
SIMPLY
COMPLICATED
S. NELSON

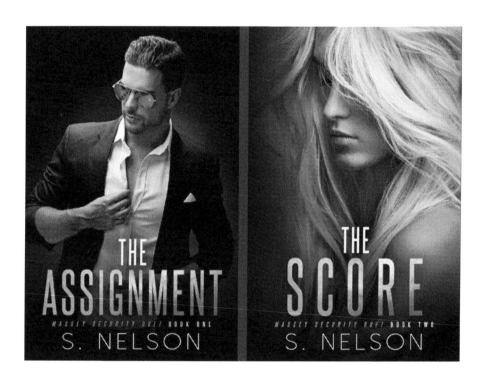

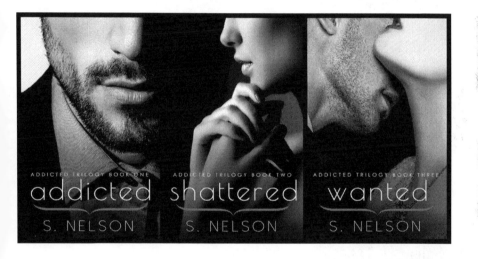

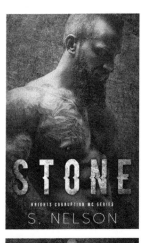

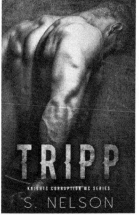

KNIGHTS
CORRUPTION
COMPLETE SERIES
S. NELSON

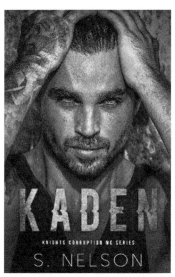

KADEN

KNIGHTS CORRUPTION MC SERIES

S. NELSON

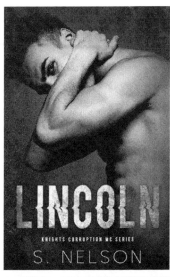

LINCOLN

KNIGHTS CORRUPTION MC SERIES

S. NELSON

ACE

KNIGHTS CORRUPTION MC SERIES

S. NELSON

BRICK

KNIGHTS CORRUPTION MC SERIES

S. NELSON